THE EXTREMELY EMBARRASSING LIFE OF LOTTIE BROOKS

KATIE KIRBY

PUFFIN

PUFFIN BOOKS

UK | USA | Canada | Ireland | Australia
India | New Zealand | South Africa

Puffin Books is part of the Penguin Random House group of companies
whose addresses can be found at global.penguinrandomhouse.com.

www.penguin.co.uk   www.puffin.co.uk   www.ladybird.co.uk

First published 2021

004

Text and illustrations copyright © Katie Kirby, 2021

The moral right of the author/illustrator has been asserted

The brands mentioned in this book are trademarks belonging to third parties

Text design by Mandy Norman
Printed and bound in Great Britain by Clays Ltd, Elcograf S.p.A.

The authorized representative in the EEA is Penguin Random House Ireland,
Morrison Chambers, 32 Nassau Street, Dublin D02 YH68

A CIP catalogue record for this book is available from the British Library

ISBN: 978–0–241–46088–7

All correspondence to:
Puffin Books
Penguin Random House Children's
One Embassy Gardens, 8 Viaduct Gardens, London SW11 7BW

For my niece Lily,
who is awesome just
the way she is

HM@ BUS
Condition of
book Noted
19.7.24

BUS

Please renew/return items by last date
shown. Please call the number below:

enewals and enquiries: 0300 1234049

xtphone for hearing or
ech impaired users: 01992 555506

.hertfordshire.gov.uk/libraries

Hertfordshire

WEDNESDAY 11 AUGUST
(DAY 19 OF THE SUMMER HOLIDAYS)

Molly has only been gone for twenty-seven and a half hours, and no one seems to have any idea how much I miss her. It feels a bit like my insides have been ripped out, sloshed around in the washing machine, then stuffed back in again.

My parents are absolutely zero help. I guess, being friendless themselves, they have no clue what it's like to have your BFF move all the way to Australia. They just say stuff like, 'You'll make plenty of new friends in no time, Lottie.'

Like, how old do they think I am? Three? It's not like it was in preschool, where you'd just bounce up to someone and say, 'Let's do gluing!' then bond instantly over a shared Pritt stick. People are mean out there!

Here's an example of how my parents treat me like a kid: we just had drive-through McDonald's for tea, as a treat to 'cheer me up', and Dad tried to order me a Happy Meal! I mean . . . what was he even thinking?!

I did manage to negotiate a Big Mac meal for myself, but the annoying thing was that it just tasted horrible and dry and got stuck in my throat. Mum said maybe it was because my taste buds were finally starting to mature, but really it's because my heart is broken. I didn't even enjoy my milkshake that much. It had already melted a bit by the time we got home and was more milky and less ice-creamy than usual, you know? Then I got sweet-and-sour sauce down the front of my favourite T-shirt and it felt like the final nail in the coffin.

Anyway, with Molly off enjoying the sun and the surfer boys Down Under, I've decided to start writing a diary, and here it is. **TA DA!**

I guess it'll feel a bit like having someone to talk to over this long, lonely summer. I'm going to illustrate it too, because I love drawing cartoons. When I'm older, I'm going to be a comic-strip artist for a newspaper or a magazine. Might as well get some practice in while I have **NOTHING ELSE TO DO**.

Here is a picture of my family.

(Note: we don't all walk around naked. It's just that drawing clothes takes SO long and TBH I can't be bothered.)

I guess, as parents go, mine aren't *too* bad – that's if you don't count them nagging me about my screen time 24/7! My grubby little seven-year-old brother is another matter though. Man, that kid is annoying. Which reminds me . . . **IF YOU ARE READING THIS, TOBY, IT IS PRIVATE PROPERTY AND I WILL GET YOU!**

Hmmm . . . What else can I tell you about myself?

Ahhh, I haven't told you about my hamsters yet, have I? Here they are!

Professor Barnaby squeakington

Fuzzball the 3rd

Sorry not very good at drawing hamsters!!!

I've had these guys for about eight months now. They live in my room and they are a bit noisy, but I don't really mind, as they give great advice. Sometimes I tell them about how bad my day was and they just keep going round on their wheel and stuffing their cheeks full of food, as if to say, 'Don't sweat the small stuff, babe. There's plenty of bigger stuff going on in the world right now!' and they are so right. They always make me feel better.

Best not to ask about what happened to Fuzzball the 1st and Fuzzball the 2nd though. RIP, guys.

So, yeh. That's my life in nutshell. I've been almost totally abandoned in this big, wide, scary world and in a few weeks I'm going to have to start high school **TOTALLY ALONE**. Oh, and my name is Lottie Brooks. And I live by the sea in Brighton, in the UK. And I'm eleven and three quarters. I guess you might like to know that too.

THURSDAY 12 AUGUST

I suppose you're wondering why I only have one friend?
Or maybe not, as pieces of paper don't really wonder
about things . . . But I'll tell you anyway, as that's what
you're here for, right?

When I was four years old, I had to wear a patch to
correct a lazy eye. I quite liked it at first. I used to
pretend I was a pirate sailing the seven seas in search
of buried treasure, and I called myself Matey McLobster
Legs, which I thought was pretty funny.

That all changed when I started primary school though.
I told some of my classmates about being Matey
McLobster Legs, and the nickname stuck. Soon everyone
was making fun of me. First it was my patch, then it was
my clothes, then my freckles, then the way I spoke . . .
I just never seemed to get it right.

There was one girl called Eliza, who had perfect plaits every day, and she was the worst. She spread lots of horrible rumours about me.

None of it was even true. Eliza made it all up. (Mum said I was fully potty-trained by two and a half!)

I felt so lonely and confused. Why didn't people like me? Why did I have to be the only kid in the class with an eyepatch? And just how did Eliza get her plaits so damn neat?!

Then Molly joined our school and everything changed. I don't know what I would have done without her. On her first day, she plonked down next to me with her Minnie Mouse lunchbox, offered me a Wotsit and told Eliza-with-the-perfect-plaits to leave me alone. Molly was so funny and confident that she could have been friends with anyone, but she chose me.

Look at how cute we were back then.

#Loveatfirstwotsit ♥

From that moment, we were inseparable **#BFFS4EVA!**

But now Molly's gone, and I'm so scared about what I'm going to do without her.

You see, other kids have things going for them – like being loud or sporty or drop-dead gorgeous. Me? I just go bright red whenever anyone talks to me. I spend most of my free time alone, drawing silly cartoons, and that's not exactly cool, is it? I also have the most mundane mid-brown hair in the entire history of the world. If I'm honest, I'm pretty sure my hair's to blame for most of my problems. I'd do anything to swap hair with Molly. She has lovely red curls – but the funny thing is that she hates her hair too! I don't know. Maybe we always hate what we've got? Mum says I'm beautiful, but you can't trust parents to be objective. She'd probably say that if I was an actual potato.

It's all very well saying that I'll make plenty of friends soon, but what my parents don't realize is that most people don't really *want* to be friends with a potato. I mean, what have potatoes got going for them? I suppose they can become chips, and chips are good . . . but I'm not sure that chips make for great conversationalists.

FRIDAY 13 AUGUST

WhatsApp conversation with Molly:

ME: Hey, BFF. I miss you soooooooooooooooooooo much! How's it going over there?

MOLLY: I miss you mooooooooooooore!! It's OK. Not seen any cute surfer boys yet though. They all look pretty much as they do in England ☹

ME: That sucks. You've only been there a day though, so maybe they're just hiding?!

MOLLY: I guess. It's also pretty hot, even though it's meant to be winter. No idea why my parents thought it would be a good idea to live in Australia when our family looks like a bunch of milk bottles wearing ginger wigs!

ME: I know. Did they not even think about the risk of skin cancer?!

MOLLY: Clearly not. I'll probably end up dead, and then they'll be sorry!

ME: Yeh, that'd serve them right.

MOLLY: It would!

ME: Bit extreme though . . .
I'd miss you if you were dead! 😭

MOLLY: Ahhh, I'd miss you too.
Will keep slapping on the factor 50 then (for a while at least).

ME: 👍 😊 xxx

I had thought that chatting to Molly would cheer me up, but it just made me feel sadder than ever. I can't believe her mum and dad had to ruin both of our lives for a 'really exciting new job opportunity'.

THOUGHT OF THE DAY:

Why do parents always put their own selfish career goals above their kids' friendships?!

SATURDAY 14 AUGUST

It is now Day 22 of the summer holidays and I am
officially **BORED TO DEATH**.

I mean, that may be a slight exaggeration, but still.

I wonder if it is technically possible to die of boredom?
Probably.

Nothing **AT ALL** has happened.

This afternoon I ate two slices of toast with Nutella and six Jaffa Cakes one after the other (sorry, Mum), then I felt sick and watched some contouring tutorials on YouTube. Contouring seems like a lot of effort, but the results are impressive if you have a big nose and two hours to spare each day. Dad told me off for being on YouTube too much, as apparently it will rot my brain cells. I pointed out that Toby had been playing Minecraft all day and perhaps that wasn't good for him either, and Dad said, 'Toby's only been playing for half an hour, and Minecraft is more educational than make-up tutorials, especially considering you aren't even allowed to wear make-up!'

Toby had actually been on his iPad for, like, seven hours! You should have seen the look he gave me as soon as Dad's back was turned.

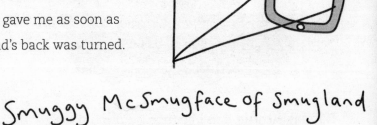

Smuggy McSmugface of Smugland

Personally, I think Dad is in denial about his parenting capabilities and would benefit from a bit of contouring himself.

7.11 p.m.

Had spag bol for dinner and it was full of carrots. I mean, it must have been about ninety-five per cent carrots. Why must parents try and put vegetables in everything? If Mum tells me one more time that carrots make you able to see in the dark, I think I shall have to flush my own head down the toilet.

I said, 'Mum, listen. I can't eat this. It's just not agreeing with my constitution.'

I thought it sounded sort of intelligent to use a big word, and it was better than saying **'Ewwwww, GROSS!'** which is what Toby does, but Mum looked like she was about to burst into tears. I don't know what's got into her lately, but she seems to be on the verge of a nervous breakdown. I mean, chill out. It's just dinner.

Dad said, 'Lottie, don't be rude. Your mum's gone to a lot

of trouble to make this lovely meal, and the least you can do is sit there and eat it nicely.'

'But, Dad, I'm sorry. I just can't. It's making me feel all queasy.'

'Give me one good reason why you can't eat your dinner, young lady.'

'Well, I've decided to go vegetarian actually!'

This is in fact something I've been considering for a while, because I *love* animals. The main problem, though, is that vegetarians aren't allowed to eat bacon, which seems terribly unfair because bacon is just **SO** delicious!

Dad said, 'That's funny, seeing as you hate eating vegetables.'

'That's not true,' I said. 'I like chips and they are a vegetable. And I like tomato sauce. So these days it's pretty easy to be a vegetarian even if you don't like vegetables! There's loads you can eat.'

'Oh, really? Like what?'

'Ummmm, margherita pizza.'

TBF I could quite happily live off margherita pizza for the rest of my life.

Anyway, the most important thing I wanted to tell you about today was that I've come up with a plan. Drum roll please!

Are you on the edge of your seat?

No?

Oh well.

Here goes . . .

THE PLAN: I am going to reinvent myself over the summer and become a new Lottie! More confident and that sort of thing, so that I can start high school and become instantly popular and worshipped by all my adoring fans!

THE REINVENTION OF LOTTIE BROOKS

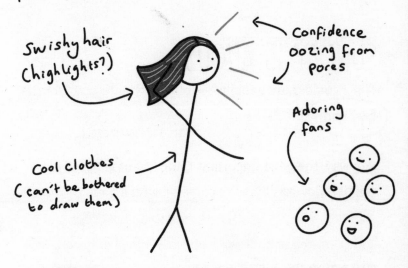

Swishy hair
(highlights?)

Confidence
oozing from
pores

Adoring
fans

Cool clothes
(can't be bothered
to draw them)

Or I'd also settle for just flying under the radar but
having someone to eat lunch with, so that I don't have
to stuff my sandwiches into my mouth as quickly as
possible then hide in the toilets for the rest of break.

Will anyone actually be able to look past my potato-ness,
my skinny legs and my complete lack of social skills?
We'll see.

SUNDAY 15 AUGUST

5.22 p.m.

Life's been pretty tough since I became an accidental vegetarian.

Today started badly. I woke up to the smell of bacon. Dad was cooking it downstairs and wafting it through the house with a magazine. 'Mmmmm, bacon!' he kept calling out. 'Sooooo crispy and delicious!'

Sometimes I don't know who's the kid and who's the grown-up around here.

I poured myself a bowl of Shreddies and pretended to really enjoy them because I didn't want to give Dad the satisfaction of thinking he had won.

'Mmmmm, Shreddies!' I said, rubbing my tummy. 'Sooooo nutritious and . . . brown.' But I don't think I really convinced anyone – especially not after I nearly choked on a particularly dry mouthful.

Unfortunately for me, Dad left a spare bit of bacon out on the kitchen counter. I tried to ignore it, but it kept winking at me. I couldn't help myself. I quickly stuffed it into a bap, covered it with ketchup and was just about to take a massive bite when Dad jumped out from behind the fridge. He'd caught me red-handed.

OH GOSH LOTTIE - NO! REMEMBER YOUR PRINCIPLES!

ARGH! WHY DO PRINCIPLES SUCK SO MUCH?!

I put that bacon bap down, thanking Dad graciously for his concern.

I didn't give up. No, not me. I don't fall at the first hurdle. I just kept plodding on and on. By teatime I realized that no meat had passed these lips for **ONE WHOLE DAY!***

*If you don't count the fact that I ate a Peperami from the fridge this afternoon without thinking . . . Oops. How much meat is even in a Peperami anyway? I mean, maybe they are just a salami-flavoured meat substitute?

Just googled it. They are 100 per cent pork, so possibly the least vegetarian thing you can eat. Dammit.

As I say though, it was an accident. So: YAY! GO, ME!

6.45 p.m.

I was doing so well. I was so proud of myself.

Then Mum went and ruined it all by shouting up the stairs, 'Lottie! I'm making chicken nuggets and chips for dinner. Do you want me to do you some broccoli, since you won't be able to eat the chicken?'

I didn't want to be difficult, so I just said, 'Oh, I guess I'll eat the chicken nuggets if you've already made them . . .'

'It's fine,' she replied. 'I've not started cooking them yet, so it's very easy to boil veg for you instead.'

'Well, I'm sure it'd just be easier for you to cook us all one dinner though. I don't mind.'

'It's no hassle, honestly. I wouldn't want you to compromise your beliefs for my sake.'

'Um . . . . nah . . . I'll just have the nuggets.'

I swear I heard her and Dad laughing!

So I'm no longer a veggie. It's not really my fault. I mean, how am I meant to pass up bacon and nuggets in one day? I'm not made of stone!

I think I'll try again in a couple of years, when I have a little bit more self-control.

THOUGHT OF THE DAY:
Why are so many delicious foods made out of meat?

MONDAY 16 AUGUST

The hammies are laying on the guilt about my poor performance as a vegetarian. It's easy for them to be judgemental though. They've never tried a Quarter Pounder, have they?!

TUESDAY 17 AUGUST

After my big reveal of **THE PLAN**, I haven't done very much about it. What I have been doing a lot of is watching TV and staring at my phone. Wait – that counts. It's research, OK!

Mum just came into the sitting room and said, 'What are you going to do today then?'

It wasn't really a question but more an accusation.

Then she said, 'Unless you are doing something super important, then perhaps you should get some fresh air by coming to help me with the shopping?'

Some parents do cool, fun stuff with their kids over the summer – things like going to Alton Towers or seeing a London musical. What do I get? Going to the supermarket! I mean, how much fresh air does Mum seriously think I'm going to get in Tesco?!

So I said, 'I am doing something pretty important actually. I am pondering how I only have thirteen followers on Instagram, while Kim Kardashian has over two hundred million.'

I mean, that's over three times the population of our entire country! Mad. Maybe if I was allowed a public profile I'd be able to give Kim a run for her money, but for the time being it looks like I'm stuck on double figures.

Mum groaned. 'If you don't get off that Insta-whatsit right now, I'll be forced to put your phone on eBay and get you a . . . What's the opposite of a smart phone? You know, one of those phones with no Wi-Fi or apps . . .'

Then Dad walked in and said, 'I've got it: a dumb phone!'

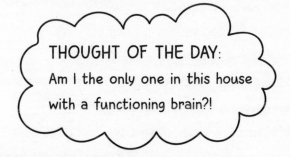

THOUGHT OF THE DAY:
Am I the only one in this house with a functioning brain?!

WEDNESDAY 18 AUGUST

Today I got dragged out for some 'nice family fun at the beach', because it's apparently 'a shame to waste such a beautiful day just sitting about indoors'.

Sitting in a dark room looking at TikTok is hardly a wasted day, is it?!

I don't think old people understand kids these days. They just remember their youth without phones or YouTube or KitKat Chunkys or . . . well, anything good at all really, and they think we should all be outside building dens and playing on rope swings. I mean, it's not 1980s any more. Kids like screen time, OK? Get with the programme.

I wouldn't even mind so much, except that they spend half their lives ignoring me while scrolling through Facebook and sharing 'hilarious' memes about how awful being a parent is. They're just **SO** hypocritical!

THURSDAY 19 AUGUST

This afternoon I was in my room, quietly minding my own business, when Mum poked her head round the door without knocking. I mean, I could have been naked!

'Hey!' I yelled. 'What have I got to do to get some privacy around here?'

'Oh, it's nothing I haven't seen before, Lottie,' she said. She was laughing.

'I'm nearly twelve, MUM!'

'OK, I'm sorry, love. Next time I'll knock. Anyway, I just popped up to tell you that I've invited Liv over to give you some advice about starting school. I know you're feeling a bit worried about how you'll fit in and make friends.'

'Oh, Mum!' I groaned.

(FYI Liv is my super-trendy thirteen-year-old next-door neighbour.)

'Oh, honey. I know you don't like me interfering, but it's not easy starting a new school. Especially not when you are shy.'

'MUM!'

I mean, could she have made me sound any more like a loser?!

'It'll be good! Liv is lovely. She said she'd be delighted to help, and she'll be here in ten minutes.'

'WHAT?!'

I could not believe my mum had invited just about the coolest person I know to come to my house in ten minutes' time.

I glanced around my room and panicked – it looked like it belonged to a six-year-old. I mean, I still had all my Sylvanian Families on display! (Just for the record – I don't play with them any more. I just quite like having them set up on top of my chest of drawers, OK.) I swept them all away – baby bunnies went flying out of the nursery, and a mini baguette from the bakery pinged me in the eye. 'Sorry, guys!' I said, as I shoved them all under the bed.

What else? My bedcovers – they have unicorns and rainbows all over them. I love unicorns and rainbows, but do high-school kids love unicorns and rainbows?! Probably not.

I covered my bed with clothes, then shoved my unicorn slippers in the wardrobe along with my collection of JoJo Siwa bows and Matty B and Justin Bieber posters.

Then I heard Mum shout, 'Lottie, Liv's here!'

And suddenly there she was, standing in my room! Liv has long brown hair with blonde balayage. She looked **SOOOOOOO** cool. Like, the coolest person I've ever seen. Or at least had a conversation with.

I said, 'I love your hair, Liv! It's gorgeous.'

'Yeh, I know,' she replied.

'Would you like a drink, Liv?'

'I'll have a coffee please.'

How sophisticated is that? She drinks coffee like a proper adult!

I made us both a coffee, and I won't lie: it tasted absolutely rancid. But I tried to sip it like a stylish Parisian nonetheless. Not quite sure I pulled it off.

Then we sat on my bed and Liv said, 'Look, high school is brutal. I'll help you as much as I can, but only in secret, OK? I'm going into Year Nine next year, and Year Nines definitely don't speak to Year Sevens.'

'OK.'

'Great. Well, first thing to know is . . . Hang on. Wait a minute. Is that a Sylvanian Family rabbit on the floor?'

I looked down and to my horror saw that Mrs Fluffy Bottom was right by my foot. 'What?' I said. 'No . . . errr . . . Well, yes, I guess it is . . . but it's not mine . . . It's my brother's. He loves those stupid things.'

Then I reached down and picked Mrs Fluffy Bottom up and lobbed her into the bin. Luckily, I didn't miss. (I shall apologize to the Fluffy Bottom family later.)

Next, Liv said, 'OMG, is that a Justin Bieber cereal bowl?'

'What? No! Errr . . . I can't believe my brother has been eating cereal in that stupid bowl in my room again!'

'Your brother sounds weird.'

'Yeh, he is.'

'So,' Liv said. 'What music are you into?'

'I . . . um . . . Well, not Justin Bieber, obviously. He's lame. I like . . . um . . .'

COME ON, BRAIN!

'I'm into grime,' said Liv.

'YES! GRIME! Me too. I mean, yep, I love a bit of grime.'

'Cool. Who's your favourite artist?'

'It's . . . errr . . . it's . . . Scratchy . . . Brian.'

SCRATCHY BRIAN?! Where on earth did I get that from?

'Weird, never heard of him . . .'

'Well, that's probably because Scratchy Brian is pretty new on the . . . block. He's quite underground right now.'

'Riiiiiiiight.'

Liv was clearly unconvinced.

So I'm not sure I made a good impression, but I was proud of myself for thinking on the spot. At least Liv is under the impression that Toby is the Sylvanian Family/ Justin Bieber fanatic and not me.

Anyway, the best thing about her coming over was that she eventually gave me loads of great advice for starting Kingswood High, and it was all really useful in relation to THE PLAN. Here's what she told me.

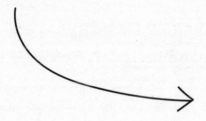

HOW NOT TO BE A LOSER IN HIGH SCHOOL

1. Your skirt should be short, but not so short that you get sent home to change.

2. Wear as much make-up as you can get away with, but not so much that anyone can tell you are actually wearing it.

3. Don't try too hard in class or you'll look like a geek, but equally don't not try either or everyone will think you are stupid.

4. Never eat the cottage pie. Someone found a rat's tail in it once.

5. Your choice of pencil case says EVERYTHING about you, so pick carefully.

6. The janitor's cupboard is haunted by the ghost of a Year Ten pupil who accidentally got locked in there for the whole summer and starved to death.

7. Do not even bother starting school if you don't have a bra.

Or I guess when I say 'really useful', what I mean is 'confusing' and, um, 'TERRIFYING'!

The worst thing is that I don't have a bra. I'm going to have to figure out how to convince Mum to buy me one, even though I have nothing to put in one . . . How am I supposed to bring that up in a conversation?! 'Oh, hi, Mum. I know I'm incredibly lacking in the chest department, but I NEED a bra or everyone at high school will think I'm a baby.'

Liv did give me her phone number and said I could text her if I ever needed any advice – but she reminded me not to approach her in public, as she'd be mortified if anyone thought we were friends. How kind is that? ☺

By the way, Liv has 157 followers on Instagram. (WOW!) I followed her, but she said she can't follow me back in case someone notices.

FRIDAY 20 AUGUST

(6.56 a.m.)

I didn't really sleep well last night, as I had a dream
that I was being chased through the school corridors by
haunted bras, distasteful pencil cases and cottage pies
filled with rats' tails. I ended up escaping through a door
that turned out to be the janitor's closet. I looked around,
terrified – and then out popped Justin Bieber. He started
serenading me with 'Love Yourself'.

It was a really bizarre dream, but I'm
glad it ended on a positive.

WhatsApp conversation with Molly:

ME: I need a bra. Urgently!

MOLLY: Have you grown breasts in the week and a half since I left?!

ME: Unfortunately not, but apparently it's a high-school MUST HAVE and I can't rely on Justin Bieber to rescue me from the flying cottage pies every time, can I?

MOLLY: Lottie, what on earth are you talking about?? 😜

ME: Long story! How are you? Any update on the hot surfer boys?

MOLLY: Sadly not. Guess what though – I made a new friend! She lives right next door. Her name is Isla and she's eleven too. Can you believe it?!

ME: Oh wow. What good luck.

MOLLY: I know! And she says she'll introduce me to all her mates at school too. How nice is that?! 😊

ME: So nice. That's great news.

It didn't feel like great news though. It just felt really odd to hear Molly talk about having a new friend already.

SATURDAY 21 AUGUST

Today I have been mostly thinking about bras again (and KitKat Chunkys, obvs). Liv has totally lucked out with her genes and has been wearing a bra since she was ten and a half. She heard that wearing a bra can make your boobs grow faster, so when she first got one she wore it 24/7 and now she's a 32B. I bet all the new Year Seven girls are already doing that and now I'm going to be even more behind!

I keep checking in the mirror, but I really don't have anything happening in that area **AT ALL**. Liv said some people are just destined to have fried eggs forever. Oh please don't let that be true!

HEY THAT'S A BIT PERSONAL

Annoying Toby had his equally annoying friend Thomas round in the afternoon. Toby was rubbing it in my face that I didn't have any friends, and the worst thing is that he's right! So that's another thing to worry about.

SO FAR ON MY LIST OF WORRIES I HAVE:

(1.) I blush when anyone speaks to me.

(2.) I have the most boring hair colour known to humankind.

(3.) My little brother is more popular than I am. How is that even fair when all he does is play Minecraft and do armpit farts?!

(4.) I have no bra.

(5.) I have no boobs to put in a bra, even if I had one.

(6.) Continuing aura of potato-ness.

Mum must have figured out something was up because she kept popping her head round my bedroom door and saying, 'Are you OK, love?'

I wasn't OK at all. I was freaking out! But I didn't tell Mum that.

At one point she brought me some Nutella on toast, but I couldn't even eat it because I was so stressed about my lack-of-bra situ. I **NEVER** turn down Nutella on toast.

I just don't know how to tell Mum what's wrong though. Sometimes I wish I was a boy. They seem to have it so much easier.

THOUGHT OF THE DAY:
Can you even wear a bra if you have literally no boob material at all?!

SUNDAY 22 AUGUST

Guess what? I finally plucked up the courage to ask Mum for a bra!

After spending so long trying to figure out the best way to do it, I ended up just blurting it out while she was stirring the chicken casserole for dinner. Sort of like, 'That smells nice, Mum. I need a bra.'

She looked a bit confused (probably because I'd complimented her casserole, which actually smelt gross). Then she said, 'Um, are you sure, darling? I think you should maybe have at least a little more, um . . . development before you get one.'

THANKS, MUM.

I had no other choice but to present her with the cold hard facts, so I said:

I mean, I'm pretty much twelve now (sort of) and everyone – literally EVERYONE – in my old class already had one. Well, nearly everyone did. None of the boys, obvs. But a few people, maybe. Most of the girls who had them didn't even need them, but that doesn't matter. As Liv said, no bra at high school = social outcast! Which is ridiculously unfair, really, but I don't make these stupid rules.

Anyway, the upshot is Mum said yes. She's taking me into town tomorrow, while Toby is at Leo's. We are going to have a nice girly day together, and she said we might even be able to go get manicures if she can get an appointment. V v v v excited! 😊

MONDAY 23 AUGUST

WARNING TO MY FUTURE SELF:
This entry is about going bra shopping with
your mum AND your seven-year-old brother,
so if you'd rather look away now and not be
reminded of this excruciating experience,
then that'd be totally understandable . . . and
highly recommended.

OMG, I just want to die writing this.

OK, here goes. Everything started to go wrong when Leo's
mum called in the morning to say that Leo had been
vomming all night, so Toby probably shouldn't go round.
We had two choices: either take Toby shopping with us,
or go another day. I mean, I was super tempted to go

another day, but there are only eleven days left until high school starts. I really can't afford to lose any more precious chest-growing hours.

But can you imagine what it's like going bra shopping for the first time with your little brother? No? Well, lucky you!

So, as soon as we got to the 'lingerie' (posh way of saying 'pants') section, Toby started running around putting bras on his head and chanting:

It was both factually incorrect and mortifying! He's seven years old going on two.

Next, Mum flagged down a shop assistant and said in her loudest voice, 'Hello, I'm here with my daughter and we'd like to get her measured for her FIRST BRA!'

I wouldn't be surprised if people heard her some place really far away, like Alaska or Birmingham. I mean, she may as well have carried a huge, flashing sign around with her.

Also, I hadn't even realized I would need to get measured, which was probably for the best because if Mum had told me that up front there's no way I'd have agreed to it. Getting half naked in front of a stranger is not that high up on my list of ways I like to spend Monday afternoons.

Luckily, the lady who did the measuring said I could keep my T-shirt on. Her name was Paula, and it turned out that Paula had the most **GIGANTINORMOUS** boobs I had EVER seen in my life. (Yes, they were so big that I needed to make up a new word to describe them.) I imagine Paula must have been a 72ZZ or something. And she was all like, 'Ahh, what a special moment!' and 'Well, I think we'll be going for a very small cup here . . .' while winking at Mum.

I just wanted to curl up in a ball and hide in the dressing-gown section.

I tried on a few different sizes and the upshot is that I'm a 28AA. Who even knew you could be a double A? It's about the only time in life when getting an A is a bad thing and an F certainly doesn't stand for fail! ☹

Still, at least I have a bra now. Well, three bras to be precise! Two plain white ones, and pale pink one that's a little bit fancier. It has a tiny bow in the middle and some pretty purple edging.

When we left the shop, I made Mum carry the bags in case anyone saw me, then we took Toby to the Lego shop to get him a little treat for 'being really good' (debatable!).

When I got home, I ran straight up to my room and put the fancy pink bra on. I felt much more mature. It was kind of funny, but I liked it. I was a bit embarrassed when I went back downstairs, in case Dad or Toby could tell, but if they noticed they didn't say anything. Well, Toby shouted 'BUTT FACE!' at me, but that's pretty standard from him.

TUESDAY 24 AUGUST

WhatsApp conversation with Molly:

ME: I AM THE OWNER OF A BRA!!!

MOLLY: SHUT UP!! No way!

ME: Pinkie promise. I'm a 28AA!
Nearly a 28A apparently*

MOLLY: So jealous! Do you
feel all grown-up now?!

ME: Yes, I feel mega sophisticated
and ready to face anything!

MOLLY: Really?

*That bit was a lie.

ME: No. It feels a bit weird actually . . . Kind of itchy. But am sure I'll get used to it.

MOLLY: Cool, gotta go . . .

ME: Oh? What you up to?

MOLLY: Asking my mum for a bra obvs!

WEDNESDAY 25 AUGUST

Eight days until school starts. I have the uniform ready
– it's hanging up in my wardrobe. Before summer I paid
careful attention to what the high-school girls hanging
about in town in the afternoons were wearing. I wanted
to make sure I had it all right, because I don't want to be
wearing the wrong type of skirt on my first day. I think
I'll have to hitch mine up a bit, but it'll do.

I even have my pencil case and pens ready. They are all
laid out neatly on my desk. Do you think it's possible that
someone might not like me based on my pencil case? It's
shaped like a slice of watermelon, but perhaps I should
have gone for something a little classier? Something like
a taco . . . I mean, it's just so hard to tell which one says
'I'm confident, cool and in control' the best.

Me trying to make
one of the biggest
decisions of
my life...
Taco vs.
Watermelon??

Maybe I should rethink the cupcake-shaped erasers too. Bit immature for high school, perhaps? Why am I asking you for opinions? Am I actually losing what is left of my mind?!

So yeh, I'm all ready, I guess. But there are things I can't change – like my face, which is just . . . I don't know how to describe it, really. A bit odd? Lopsided maybe? A bit heavy on the old forehead?

I think if I got highlights, that would distract from my face and make me look more mature. Mum said I can get highlights when I can afford to pay for them myself, and then she laughed. I looked them up online, and they are like £100! So that's never going to happen.

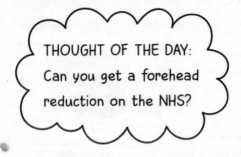

THOUGHT OF THE DAY:
Can you get a forehead
reduction on the NHS?

THURSDAY 26 AUGUST

I eventually came to the conclusion that the erasers were a tad immature, so I gave them to Toby and guess what he did? He ate them! Mum dialled 999 and the person she spoke to said to keep an eye on him and take him to A&E if he started vomiting.

I asked him why he did it, and he said the erasers smelt delicious.

'What did they taste like?' I asked.

'A bit rubbery, but OK,' he said.

I mean, seriously?!

My life is so rock 'n' roll.

MONDAY 30 AUGUST

I have been doing the whole sleeping-in-bra experiment for a week now and the results as follows.

Tuesday: No improvement.

Wednesday: A very small improvement?

Thursday: Scrap that – zero improvement.

Friday: Possible decline?

Saturday: Is my chest actually inverting?! 😬

Sunday: Still patiently waiting . . .

Monday (today): ABSOLUTELY NOTHING.

TUESDAY 31 AUGUST

9.12 a.m.

Decided to text Liv for advice.

> **ME:** Help! Am still boobless.
> School starts in two days . . . Any ideas??

> **LIV:** Pray! ☺

10.32 a.m.

Dear God, I know we don't speak much, and I'm aware
this might sound fairly selfish after my prolonged
absence, but please do you think you could make my
chest grow just a teeny bit?

10.37 a.m.

No reply from God. Looks like I'll need to take charge of
this myself.

11.17 a.m.

Googled 'How to make breasts grow'. Apparently fennel seeds should help.

12.11 p.m.

Couldn't find any fennel seeds in the kitchen. The hamster food looked quite similar though, so I tried nibbling some of that. Fuzzball the 3rd kept giving me funny looks.

I seriously can't believe the hammies eat that stuff. It tastes like dust! No wonder they begrudge me my bacon baps.

9.48 p.m.

Still no improvement. When I actually stop and think about it though, do I even want boobs? I mean, I imagine whenever my chest finally does start growing I'll just feel all awkward and strange about it anyway. What if my boobs make people stare at me? What if they grow as big as Paula's? What if they jiggle about all over the place when I run?!

I guess having the biggest boobs in the class might be just as bad as having the flattest chest.

Why is life so hard? Why does everything always have to be so confusing?

WHY WHY WHY WHY WHY?!?!?!

WEDNESDAY 1 SEPTEMBER

Been feeling sick all day. I literally cannot believe that it is possible to feel so scared about starting high school. What is wrong with me? I must be a very pathetic human being. Either that or I am actually sick. Maybe I have the flu? Maybe I've caught some sort of horrible disease? I was followed around by a rather manky-looking one-legged seagull outside Tesco the other day . . .

(FYI I have no idea if the seagull's name was actually Elton. It just seemed to suit him.)

3.23 p.m.

I shouted down to Mum that I thought I might be dying of a rare undiscovered bird disease. She came up and took my temperature, then said that I was fine.

Feel quite disappointed, as I wouldn't have had to go to school tomorrow if I was dying.

I just don't understand how, in a school with over a thousand pupils, you are meant to find your classroom. What happens if you get lost? Do you get detention? I don't want to get into trouble when I've barely even started.

9.11 p.m.

I think Mum figured out that I was feeling nervous, as she did the whole 'You'll make plenty of new friends in no time, and you just have to be brave and be yourself, blah blah blah' thing again . . . But what she doesn't realize is that being myself is part of the problem!

She did bring Nutella on toast and a hot chocolate up to my room though. I think that helped a bit.

Before getting into bed, I had a bath and washed my hair. Mum let me use some of her expensive coconut oil conditioning treatment too. I might have failed to convince my parents to get me highlights as per **THE PLAN**, but at least I will have smooth, swishy hair tomorrow. I put **LOADS** on to make sure it was super shiny.

9.35 p.m.

Got a message.

> **MOLLY:** Good luck tomorrow, Lotts!
> I know you'll smash it. Love you xxx

> **ME:** Thanks. I hope so!
> Love you too xxx

I really wish I could share Molly's confidence.

THURSDAY 2 SEPTEMBER

So today was D-Day.

Dad was up first. 'BIG DAY FOR MY LITTLE LOTTIE
POTTY!' he boomed through my door.

Sometimes I literally want the ground to swallow me up.
I don't think Dad understands that I'm actually going to
be a teenager in a year (and a bit).

'IT'S LOTTIE! JUST LOTTIE!' I shouted back.

'Lottie. Yep, sorry. I got ya!'

I got up and looked in the mirror – and was horrified to
discover that my hair was a greasy, flat mess! It looked
like I had rubbed a block of butter into it. Why do I never
look like those ladies in the shampoo adverts? WHY?!

I spent twenty minutes trying to get my hair to go right,
but no matter what I did it just looked crap.

I contemplated washing it again, but I didn't have time.

Went downstairs and Mum and Dad had laid out a really nice breakfast for me. I had one spoonful of Coco Pops and felt sick.

Then they tried to make me have a 'first day of school' photo by the front door. I knew they were just going to put it up on Facebook with a gushy, over-the-top, vomit-worthy comment about how big I'd grown, so I made sure I did my best scowl.

Laura Brooks

First day at High School! look how big our Lottie potty's got!

👍 😊 39 people like this

When I arrived at school, I was struck by a fresh wave of fear. It just looked so HUGE! I got really scared thinking about how I was going to find my way to my lessons without getting lost . . . Maybe primary school wasn't so bad after all.

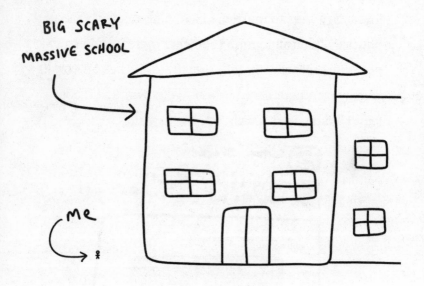

BIG SCARY MASSIVE SCHOOL

ME

I did get to my form room OK though. I'm going to be in Seven Green, and no one from my old school is in my class – it was a small school, and everyone went to a whole bunch of different places. Molly would have been with me if she hadn't moved away, but I tried really hard not to think about that.

I stood outside the door to my form room and thought about **THE PLAN** and how I needed to hold my head up high and walk into the room like I belonged there. But, as I pushed open the door, any confidence I had left melted away.

It was clear lots of the kids already knew each other, and they were crowded around the desks, chatting and laughing.

I started feeling really shy and had no idea what to do with my hands. I kept hearing Mum in my ear saying, 'Stop chewing your sleeves, Lottie! You have no idea how much those blazers cost!'

I quickly scanned the room and found a spare seat near the front of the class.

As I sat down, there was a whole lot of commotion over by the door. It swung open and in walked two girls – one with blonde hair and the other with the shiniest black hair I have ever seen. Everyone started saying hi and hugging them. I couldn't help but stare. They were both absolutely beautiful. Arm in arm, they walked to the back of the room.

'Would you mind moving?' the blonde one said to a couple of boys who were already sitting there. It was more of an order than a question. 'We always sit in the back row,' she said.

To my amazement, the boys just gathered their things and left.

Then our form tutor, Mr Peters, arrived. It felt a bit strange, as I've never had a man for a teacher before. He was younger than I had imagined and had nice, kind eyes. The first thing he said was, 'Hello, class. I'm so excited to be your form tutor this year. I'm new here too – this is my first year at Kingswood High – so please go easy on me.' Then he gave a nervous laugh. I didn't know teachers got nervous too!

Next, he said, 'So we can all get to know each other a bit better, I thought we'd go round the class and each of us would say a little something about ourselves.'

I wanted to run right out of the room. Doing this sort of activity is my absolute **WORST NIGHTMARE**! First, because it involves speaking in front of people, and second, because I don't have anything even vaguely impressive to say about myself.

'I'll go first: I'm Mr Richard Peters, and at the weekends I like to go wakeboarding,' said Mr Peters. 'Who'd like to go next?'

'I will!'

I spun round. It was the blonde girl in the back row.

'Hi, I'm Amber Stevens,' she said, 'and this is my BEST friend, Poppy Mills. We've been BFFs since reception class. I can do the splits, and when I grow up I want to be a professional gymnast or a vet.'

She flashed a big smile and flicked her glossy hair behind her shoulder. I'm sure she has her hair highlighted. No fair.

Poppy introduced herself next. She told the class that she's Vietnamese and wants to be a pop star or a biologist. How glamorous!

The introductions moved slowly round the room and everyone else seemed so interesting. I got more and more panicky as it went from person to person.

'Hello, everyone, I'm Jess,' said a girl who had her hair tied up in bunches with cool neon bands. 'I've just moved to the area. My family is Jamaican, and I can do a hundred keepy-uppies on a good day!'

She looked lovely and smiley. I wondered if being new here meant she'd be up for making friends soon.

Amber — Confident

Poppy — Cute

Jess — Super Cool

When it was my turn, I looked down at the floor, hoping they'd miss me out, but Mr Peters wasn't having any of it.

'Tell us all something interesting about yourself, Charlotte,' he said.

So I said – and I'm cringing SO badly as I write this – 'My name is Lottie, and I like eating KitKat Chunkys.' And then everyone started sniggering, and I went as red as a strawberry (or TBH a KitKat Chunky wrapper). Facepalm! I mean, who gives their favourite chocolate bar as the most interesting thing about themselves?!

For the rest of the day, people kept calling me KitKat Chunky, and I have only myself to blame.

When lunchtime arrived (the part of the day I was dreading the most) I saw Amber and Poppy heading towards the canteen, chatting. People just waved and moved out of their way as they walked past – it was almost like they were models in a catwalk show. When they got to the lunch queue, they just went right up to a group of girls at the front and pushed in. The craziest thing was that no one even seemed to care!

After seeing that, I couldn't face going in. I would have felt SO awkward sitting on my own. Instead I ate my cheese sandwiches perched on the loo. I tried to distract myself by scrolling through Instagram, but that just made me feel even worse. All I could think about was how I'd only been in school three hours and had already messed up THE PLAN. It was just like being back at primary school with perfect-plaits Eliza and the other mean girls.

OMG, I'm Matey McLobster Legs all over again! At least no one's said I smell like wee (yet).

I wish so badly that I could be more like Amber and Poppy. They won't have any problems making new friends. It must be so nice to be that popular.

When I got home, Mum was all like, 'How was your day?'

Why do parents always have to be so intrusive? I mean what does she want me to say? 'Oh yeh, Mum, it was really great. I got a new nickname already: KitKat Chunky. It's a funny story. I'll fill you in later. I made absolutely zero friends, went bright red eight times and got laughed at thirteen times. I ate my sandwiches in a toilet cubicle, and they tasted horrible because the cheese had gone all warm and melty from the sun, which was also too hot and made my hair **EVEN GREASIER** than it had been this morning. Oh, and your coconut hair-conditioning treatment has made me smell like a Bounty bar, and I really hate Bountys! So yeh, it was a pretty good day all round. Thanks for asking!'

What I actually said was 'Fine' to stop the onslaught of further questioning.

THOUGHT OF THE DAY:
Maybe I could run away and join a travelling circus?! I've always been quite good at hula-hooping . . .
I'm certainly not letting anyone throw knives at me while blindfolded though.

FRIDAY 3 SEPTEMBER

7.46 a.m.

Woke up to a new Instagram post from Molly:

14 Likes
 # livingmybestlife

I mean, how can I compete with that? I have English and RE, and she's off surfing at Bondi Beach! I wonder if she'll forget all about me now that she has a new, exciting life Down Under. Molly's so cool and confident, I know she'll make tons of friends super quickly . . . Then I guess she'll have no time left for me. 😞

I hate feeling jealous of her, but sometimes it's really hard not to.

4.56 p.m.

By the time I got to school this morning I was feeling pretty down. Then in registration Mr Peters announced that the school was having a Year Seven autumn disco in November. There were already posters up all around the school, and everyone was buzzing about it.

Amber and Poppy were practically bursting with excitement, and Mr Peters had to tell them off three times for talking while he was trying to take the register – they were busy discussing what hairstyles they were going to have.

I smiled and tried to look happy, but everyone knows discos are only fun if you have friends. I guess I'll just have to think of a really good excuse not to go.

I spent all break and lunchtime wandering around on my own again.

And now for the worst bit . . .

In the afternoon we had PE and guess what? Liv was wrong. NOT everyone in Year Seven wears bras at all! Lots of the girls were still wearing crop tops and vests, so I ended up feeling really self-conscious anyway. And then the most mortifying thing EVER happened. Amber said, 'Isn't it funny how some people wear bras when they don't even need them?'

I started trying to get my shirt on as quickly as possible.

Then Poppy said, 'Surprised you wear a bra, KitKat Chunky. I didn't even know they made them that small!'

And then everyone started giggling.

I just wanted the ground to swallow me up whole. Jess tried to give me a sympathetic smile but it didn't help and this time I didn't even go red – I went beetroot.

I was basically a flat-chested beetroot wearing a bra!

Apparently Amber is a 30A already. It must be amazing to have boobs. (Although TBH hers didn't seem very visible either . . .)

So the upshot is that I got a bra because I was worried everyone would make fun of me for not having one, but now that I have one people are making fun of me for not needing one.

THERE IS LITERALLY NO WAY TO WIN!!!!! ☹

The only good thing is that it's Friday, so no more school for two days. **HURRAH!**

11.53 p.m.

I can't get to sleep. It feels like everything is going wrong. I wish Molly was here. I miss her so much.

12.27 a.m.

WhatsApp conversation with Molly:

ME: Molly?

MOLLY: Lottie! What are you doing up? Isn't it the middle of the night there?

ME: Yes. I just wanted to chat. School's not going too great . . .

MOLLY: Oh no, what's happened?

ME: Um. Where to start? I'm a flat-chested beetroot, every time I speak something stupid comes out of my mouth, and I really should have bought the taco-shaped pencil case.

MOLLY: 😅

ME: Don't laugh! This is serious stuff. I'm really worried that Matey McLobster Legs is coming back!

MOLLY: SORRY. I didn't mean to laugh, but I don't think you realize how funny you are, Lottie! Try and chill out though. It's been two days – I bet everyone is feeling exactly the same! Plus taco pencil cases are SO last season . . .

ME: How do you always manage to make me feel better?

MOLLY: Er . . . because I'm awesome?!

ME: You totally are x

MOLLY: PS Just for the record, I will always love Matey McLobster Legs

SATURDAY 4 SEPTEMBER

I had a lie-in this morning and woke up feeling much better about everything.

When I got up, Mum announced that tonight we were all going out for a 'nice family meal' at Pizza Express. I love the way my parents always say 'nice' before things they want us to do together, like some sort of threat. Anyway she said that it was to celebrate me doing 'so well' at my new school (debatable) and also because they had some exciting news to share with us.

Toby and I naturally spent the rest of the morning trying to guess what the news could be. Here are some of our ideas:

* a trip to New York

* a trip to Disneyland

* a pocket-money increase to
  £100 a month

* an unlimited-access pick-and-mix
  sweets station in our house

* a Lamborghini (each)

* a pet meerkat (each)

* a pet unicorn (each)

* McDonald's for dinner every night
  for a year

* Front-row tickets to a Justin
  Bieber concert

* 1 a.m. bedtime

* our own slushy machine

* slides going from our beds into a heated swimming pool in the garden.

SO EXCITED TO FIND OUT WHAT IT IS!!!!!!!!!!!

(9.23 p.m.)

If everything was bad before, now it's beyond bad. In fact, it's beyond awful. It's super-double-extra-awful bad with a cherry on top. It's an ice-cream sundae consisting of the worst possible flavours you can think of – something like sweaty socks and blue cheese with snot sauce and dandruff sprinkles.

OK, I've grossed myself out now so I'll get to the point.

By the time we got to the restaurant Toby and I were on the edge of our seats with anticipation. Mum and Dad said we could order whatever we liked, so I started thinking that perhaps we had won the lottery.

When the waitress came over, I said, 'I'll have double dough balls and a pepperoni pizza with extra pepperoni and a large Coke please.'

Dad didn't even bat an eyelid at 'double dough balls' and he's usually the one suggesting we share mains.

While we were eating our starters, Dad did a sort of nervous cough and said, 'So, we wanted to take you out to tell you our exciting news. There are going to be some quite big changes in our household soon!'

Toby started bouncing up and down.

I couldn't help myself. I shouted, 'OH MY GOD, I KNEW IT! WE'VE ACTUALLY WON THE LOTTERY, HAVEN'T WE?!'

'YES!' shouted Toby. 'CAN I GET A BLUE LAMBO?'

'PLEASE CAN WE GO SHOPPING IN NYC!' I squealed, jumping out of my seat.

Then I realized the restaurant had gone dead quiet and everyone was staring at us. I sat back down again.

Mum looked really surprised. 'Um . . . errr . . . no, kids. That's not it, I'm afraid. What Dad and I actually wanted to tell you was that . . . well, we're having a baby! You are going to be a big brother and sister! How exciting is that?'

Do you know what a tumbleweed moment is? Where everything goes super silent and awkward? Well, that's exactly what was happening here. Toby and I just sat there, our mouths wide open, for what seemed like a million years.

When I finally managed to speak, I said, 'WHAT? HOW?!'

Mum laughed. 'Come on, Lottie – you know all about the birds and bees. We can go through it again, if you like? When a mummy and a daddy love each other very much –'

I quickly interrupted so I didn't have to hear any more.

Toby said, 'Babies are rubbish. I wanted to go to Disneyland.' Then he carried on stuffing dough balls into his mouth like nothing had happened.

Mum and Dad looked quite upset, but I mean, OMG, seriously! What kind of response were they hoping for?!

The rest of the meal was pretty quiet. They mumbled on about how the baby would complete the family, and how much we'd love him or her when he or she finally arrived.

All I kept thinking was, *What about me? What about Toby? Are we not enough for them any more?*

Everything seems to be changing lately except for me.

10.43 p.m.

WhatsApp conversation with Molly:

ME: Worst news ever.

MOLLY: WHAT?!?!?

ME: Are you sitting down?

MOLLY: Yep!

ME: Do you have a bucket?

MOLLY: No, what would I need a bucket for?

ME: Well, you may feel the need to vomit.

MOLLY: OK, hang on a sec.

Five minutes pass.

ME: WHERE ARE YOU?!

MOLLY: Sorry, I couldn't find a bucket. I do have the bin from under my desk though.

ME: That'll have to do.

MOLLY: Come on – what are you talking about?! JUST TELL ME!!

ME: OK. My mum is . . . pregnant!

MOLLY: OMG!!

ME: I know.

MOLLY: That means they must have been . . . DOING IT!!

ME: I know.

MOLLY: That's disgusting!

ME: I know.

MOLLY: But they are so old!!!

ME: That's what I said! 🤮

THOUGHT OF THE DAY:
Why couldn't my parents have just got a puppy instead, like a NORMAL family?

SUNDAY 5 SEPTEMBER

The rest of the weekend was dull. Since sharing the 'exciting news', Mum just looks tired and miserable.

Apparently part of the problem is that she can't drink any wine now that she's pregnant –which is kind of hard for her, as we all know how **OBSESSED** with it she is.

Dad says we ought to be being kind to Mum and helping her around the house more because growing a baby is hard work, but what he doesn't seem to remember is that being eleven and three quarters is also really hard work!

Plus I'm absolutely dreading going back to school tomorrow.

Now it seems like I'm not wanted at school or at home. 😣

MONDAY 6 SEPTEMBER

Well, today went better than expected, because not one
but two **REALLY** good things happened.

(1.) On the way in to school I saw the most beautiful boy-
human I have **EVER SEEN** in my life. He had floppy
sandy-brown hair and big brown eyes, and was with a
big group of friends. As I walked past I heard one of them
say, 'Hey, Theo, see you at footie later!'

I kept turning the name over in my mouth.

Theo. Thhhhhheo. **THEO!**

What a perfect name. Sooooooooo refined.

I decided to nickname him Beautiful Theo, because he's
beautiful and er, yeh, called Theo (in case you didn't get
that bit yet).

Beautiful
  Theo
(AKA the most
perfect human
I have EVER
   Seen)

(Note: since I'm not that great at drawing people, you may not be able to tell from this picture just how good-looking he actually is. You'll just have to take my word for it, OK? He's **REALLY** cute. Honest!)

②In registration I felt a little nudge from behind and Jess (you remember the girl with the cool neon hairbands, right?) passed me a note. I've stuck it in here for you:

Hey KitKAT
    girl,
I like kitkats too
 — you want to
eat lunch together?
    Jess X

I was **SO** happy. I was trying not to seem too pathetic, so I didn't write back: **_YES PLEASE I AM DESPERATE HERE!_**

Instead I kept it short and simple, but I did add a little pic:

When I turned back round to pass it to her, she gave me the biggest smile. It felt really good to have someone smile like that, just for me. She also giggled at my drawing, so I think that's a good sign, right?

Later on, when I got to the canteen, I felt all nervous that Jess was probably just joking about sitting with me, but then I saw her at a table with a free seat next to her and she waved me over. We started to eat our sandwiches.

(Mine were Marmite, but hers were coronation chicken. I know – sophisticated, right?!)

'So,' she said, 'how come you don't really know anyone here?'

'I do!' I started to protest. 'Well, I used to anyway . . . My best friend, Molly, just moved to Australia. How about you?'

'We just moved here. My dad got a new job, so I had to leave all my friends behind.'

'That's totally what happened to Molly! It sucks when parents do that. You must have been really sad?'

'I was pretty sad at first, but it seems OK here.' She paused and looked down nervously. 'I was hoping maybe we could hang out together?'

'I'd LOVE that!' I said (perhaps a bit too enthusiastically).

When I got home, Mum asked how my day was again, and instead of just saying 'fine' I decided to tell her.

Well, not everything. Not about Theo.

'I think I made a new friend, Mum. She's called Jess, and she wears neon bands in her hair and eats coronation chicken sandwiches.'

'That's great, Lottie!' Mum said, smiling.

So the upshot of today is . . .
I HAVE A FRIEND!
I HAVE A FRIEND!
I HAVE A FRIEND!
I HAVE A FRIEND!
LA LA LA LA LAAAAAAAAAA!

Well, I *possibly* have a friend. And I *definitely* have a crush!

THOUGHT OF THE DAY:
Remember to play it cool.
You don't want to scare people.

Just googled the name Theo and this is what I found: The name Theo is a boy's name of Greek origin meaning 'gift of God'.

Wow. How fitting!

TUESDAY 7 SEPTEMBER

'So, what sort of stuff are you into?' Jess asked me at lunchtime today.

I always panic when people ask me that, because I don't really have any interesting hobbies – unless you count obsessively watching YouTube. That's something I'm really, really committed to. I thought about telling her I was into grime, but then I decided it felt kind of OK to tell her the truth. 'I like reading, drawing and unicorns. And it's a bit embarrassing, but I also really like . . . Justin Bieber.'

She giggled. 'Do you want to know something REALLY embarrassing? I collect Sylvanian Families.'

'No way! So do I!' I didn't tell her that I still play with them sometimes.

'Maybe we should compare collections one day?'

'That'd be great.'

Just then Beautiful Theo sauntered past us. I say
sauntered, as it's important – he doesn't walk or creep
or stumble like other people do. He moves with purpose,
like he has a right to be there and to be seen. I must have
drifted off and started gawping at him, as I heard a voice
trying to get my attention.

'Lottie! Lottie! Earth to Lottie!' It was Jess.

'Sorry! I just . . .'

'What's up with you?' she asked.

'Didn't you see him?'

'See who?'

'WHO?!'

'Yes. Who?'

'The gift of God.'

'What?!'

'I mean . . . I mean . . . Beautiful Theo.'

'Who, what, where?'

'There! The one with the floppy hair and the . . . eyes.'

Jess followed my gaze, then raised her eyebrows.

'Ohhhhhhhh . . .' she said. 'I see . . .'

We both sat there gawping.

'Is it just me,' I said, 'or does he radiate sunbeams?'

'No, it's not just you. He definitely does.'

'Thought so.'

(8.12 p.m.)

JESS: You going to go to that stupid autumn disco thing?

ME: Probably not. It does sound pretty cringe.

JESS: Yeh, it'll probably be really rubbish . . . but I guess it could be OKish if we went together?

ME: Yeh, I think that could be OKish too.

JESS: Let's do it ☺

ME: ARGHHHHH WHAT SHALL WE WEAR?!?!?!?

JESS: ARGHHHHH I DUNNO!!!!!!!!!!

So, I am going to the disco after all. I feel a little bit like a modern-day Cinderella!

I'm excited but also kinda nervous, mostly because I don't have a single item of clothing in my wardrobe that says, 'I'm right at home at a high-school disco!' I mean, at school you are safe(ish) because everyone is in uniform, but when you put us all together in our own clothes it's so exposing. You really get to know a person!

Once in primary we had a non-uniform day, and this girl called Izzy came wearing a Frozen T-shirt, even though she was eight years old. For the next three years, people sang 'Do You Want to Build a Snowman?' every time they saw her.

I know I should be asleep, but I really needed to WhatsApp Molly.

ME: Guess what!!!

MOLLY: Ummmm, you've got a new boyfriend and he's as hot as Liam Payne?

ME: No, silly. I wish. But I do have a new crush. I don't know his full name, so I just call him Beautiful Theo. 😍 AND I made a new friend called Jess. She's really nice and very funny. You'd love her! AND the school is having an autumn disco, and me and Jess are going together, which is a big relief as I was too scared to go on my own!

MOLLY: *Typing . . .*

MOLLY: *Typing . . .*

ME: You still there?!

MOLLY: Yeh, sorry. That's cool.
Sounds like you're having lots of fun!

ME: It's OK. Things are getting
better anyway. How are things with you?

MOLLY: AMAZING! Isla's introduced
me to EVERYONE at school, and I already
feel like I've been living here for years.

ME: Oh wow . . . Well, I'm
really happy for you.

I was trying to sound happy, but it was hard to hear
about what a fabulous time Molly was having without
me. My news about having ONE friend was nowhere near
as exciting as hers.

MOLLY: Thanks. Anyway, gotta go.
I've got another surf lesson. I'm
getting quite good, you know. Plus
my instructor Brad is super HOT! 😎

ME: OK cool. Have fun, bestie. Glad you're enjoying it over there. Don't forget me though!

MOLLY: I won't. Don't forget me either!

ME: NEVER! Love ya xx

MOLLY: Me too x

After our chat, I felt a little down. Molly's got this amazing new life in Oz, full of gorgeous, trendy surfer types – and what have I got? ☹

At least I do have one friend though . . . maybe.

WEDNESDAY 8 SEPTEMBER

Oh. My. Life.

Beautiful Theo is in my drama class. I can't quite work out if this is a good thing or a bad thing.

On the plus side, I get to spend fifty minutes a week staring into (or at least *at*) his big, beautiful brown eyes.

On the minus side, the sight of him turns me to jelly and I can hardly string a sentence together in his presence.

Luckily, today we just did a few group exercises. Our teacher, Mrs Lane, also talked to us about what we'd be doing for the year, but this didn't bode well for me as drama is basically all about getting up and speaking/dancing/singing in front of other people, AKA my worst nightmare!

THURSDAY 9 SEPTEMBER

Today I arrived early for PE so that I could get changed quickly before anyone else arrived. I didn't want anyone drawing attention to my bra again – or, more accurately, to the lack of anything in it.

Once I was changed, I sat on the bench and listened to the other girls chattering. Mostly it was just Amber and Poppy, as they are the loudest, and they were having a really interesting convo.

'Have you noticed how hairy Mia is?' Amber said to Poppy in a fake whisper that everyone could hear.

'I KNOW. So gross!' said Poppy. 'Imagine being that hairy and not shaving your legs. I mean, what is she even thinking?!'

Alarm bells started to ring in my head. *BRIIIIIIIING!* LOTTIE, JUST ALERTING YOUR ATTENTION

TO ANOTHER THING YOU ARE MESSING UP!
BRIIIIING!

'What do you think, KitKat Chunky?' Amber turned to me. 'Don't you think it's weird not to shave your legs at our age?'

PANIC. What was she asking me for?!

Also, what did she mean by 'our age'?

TBH I had never thought about shaving my legs before. I didn't even know it was a thing. Well, I knew it was a *thing*, but I didn't think I needed to bother about it right now. I thought surely it was for older girls? I mean, we're only eleven . . .

How am I meant to keep up with all this stuff?

I didn't want Amber or Poppy to know any of that though, so I just said, 'Yeh. So . . . weird . . .' and then sort of scooched away so they couldn't see that I didn't shave my legs.

I couldn't think about anything else ALL day, so my lessons were a complete waste of time.

As soon as I got home, I ran straight up to my room. I have never really noticed my leg hair before, but when I examined my legs closely I discovered that, in actual fact, **I AM A GORILLA!**

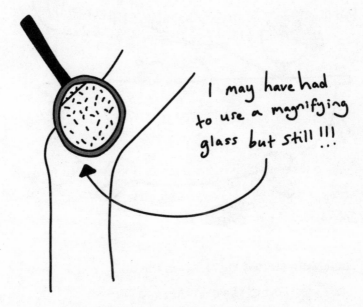

I may have had to use a magnifying glass but still !!!...

So this evening I told Mum I was going to have a 'nice relaxing bath' and once I had shut the bathroom door I took one of Dad's ancient-looking razors out of the cabinet. *How hard can it be, right?* I thought.

Pretty hard, it turns out!

I mean, I don't want to get too graphic, but it looked like I'd massacred my hamsters in the bathtub. I felt all queasy and faint, and started worrying that I might actually bleed to death.

Then Mum started knocking on the door. 'You've been in there ages, Lottie,' she said. 'Are you OK?'

In the end I had to let her in.

'Lottie, what's wrong?' she said when she saw my face. 'You're as white as a ghost!'

'I've, um . . . I've . . . murdered my legs!' I said, then burst into tears.

She surveyed the kill scene. 'I wish you'd have said something. I could have helped!'

After I was out of the bath, she helped patch up my poor, butchered legs and made me a nice hot chocolate. We had a chat, and she explained that I didn't need to get rid of the hairs on my legs for anybody else. She said that hair was perfectly normal and natural, but if I felt uncomfortable about it and wanted to remove it then she'd help me to do it properly.

'It is making me feel kind of funny,' I admitted, and Mum said she'd get me some hair-removal cream tomorrow (apparently that's a safer option than Dad's manky razors) and we'd sort it out together.

Maybe I don't say it that much, but just for the record I do **REALLY** love my mum.

Before I went to bed I sent Molly a message just to warn her not to make the same mistake:

ME: Do not – I repeat, DO NOT – shave your legs on a whim with a razor purchased in 1995. It does not end well!

Don't hate the player, hate the game!

FRIDAY IO SEPTEMBER

Jess noticed the plasters on my legs right away. 'Did you trip up?' she said.

I felt like just saying yes, but there is something about Jess that makes you feel like telling her the truth. No matter how bad it is.

'Oh, uh . . . no. I . . . well, it's a bit embarrassing, really, but I had a little accident trying to shave my legs last night.'

She laughed. 'I don't get it. Why bother? It's way too much hassle!'

'Amber and Poppy said –'

'Who cares what they think? Let them get on with it, but I've got better things to do with my time.'

I was stunned. I mean, imagine not caring what anyone thinks of you?! Imagine having better things to do with your time! Mind = blown.

After school, Mum came up to my room and said, 'I got some hair-removal cream from the shops, if you want me to show you how to use it.'

'Thanks, Mum,' I replied, 'but I think I'll wait a little while, as I'm not sure I really need to yet. Did you know that Jess doesn't shave her legs because she has better things to do with her time?'

'Well, I think Jess sounds great. Maybe you could invite her over?'

'Yes, maybe I will.'

Now, I don't feel worried like I usually do right before I go to sleep. Instead I'm feeling kind of good about stuff. ☺

SATURDAY 11 SEPTEMBER

As we were eating our dinner, Mum said to me and Toby, 'So that we can all get excited about the new baby, Dad and I thought that perhaps you two would like to help name it?'

Funnily enough, a great idea popped right into my head.

I know let's call it Dave!

Mum and Dad didn't seem too keen.

Why did they ask me, if they didn't want to hear my suggestions?

SUNDAY 12 SEPTEMBER

7.23 a.m.

I didn't sleep well last night. I couldn't get Baby Dave out of my head. I dreamt that he was born wearing a suit and looking like an estate agent. It was all kinds of freaky.

Hello I'm Dave and I've got a lovely 3 bed semi to show you today with off road parking for 2 cars!!

5.26 p.m.

Sometimes growing up is the absolute worst.

Mum just came into my room, sat down on my bed and did this kind of serious smile face, which means 'I want to talk to you about something that I know you don't want to talk to me about'. It's the same face she made before we had the 'Where do babies come from?' talk, so you can imagine my hackles went right up. **UH-OH.** No thanks, Mum, I'm really not up for discussing the intricacies of how babies are made with you again. It was painful enough the first time!

'Hi, darling, I bought you this today,' she said, carefully placing some roll-on deodorant on the bed.

'Are you trying to tell me something?' I asked.

'No, darling, you smell as sweet as roses to me. It's just that you seem to be growing up so quickly lately . . . what with getting your first bra –'

'MUM!'

'And shaving your legs –'

'MUM!'

'And soon you might start to feel more comfortable
wearing deodorant, but it's TOTALLY up to you, of course.
Did you know that I started my period when I was twelve?'

'MUM!'

OMG, why was she telling me this stuff?!

'Puberty happens to us all, darling,' she went on. 'It's
nothing to be embarrassed about.'

I felt my cheeks get hot. It was SO embarrassing!
I literally cannot cope with puberty chat – it is
ALL THE CRINGE. I thought, *If she starts going on
about my journey into womanhood, I'm going to die.*

'NO WAY!' I said. 'Actually, Mum, I've decided to age backwards instead. I want to be seven again. Life was much simpler then. I am absolutely, categorically NOT going to become a woman, because guess what? PUBERTY MASSIVELY SUCKS!'

'Oh, Lottie, stop being so dramatic!' Mum was clearly trying to suppress a laugh.

'AND IT'S NOT FUNNY!'

'OK, I know. I'm sorry, sugarplum. I've put some sanitary pads in your underwear drawer, just in case you need them when I'm not around. I'll say no more about it – unless you want to talk about it, and then . . . Well, I'll always be here to answer questions.'

'Well, I won't have any questions because, as I say, I shan't be partaking in any journeys into womanhood, thank you very much!'

'What if we go past the McDonald's drive-through on the way?'

'MUM!'

She just ruffled my hair, gave me a kiss on the forehead, then walked out.

I sniffed my armpits. TBF I couldn't really smell anything at all, but maybe I'm just used to my own stench? I really do think Mum's trying to tell me that I smell . . .

Bras, periods, leg hair, boys and BO! There is so much to think about. Sometimes I want to grow up quickly, and other times I wish I was playing happily on the carpet with My Little Ponies.

Ugh, maybe all will become clear when I turn twelve. **FINGERS CROSSED!**

MONDAY 13 SEPTEMBER

Jess came round after school today. My entire family did their best to try to destroy my one friendship by being their most embarrassing selves.

First, Mum was way over the top.

'OH, JESS! How lovely to meet you. Lottie's told us SO MUCH about you.' (Not true.) 'We are SO glad she has a new friend!'

Jess said, 'Thanks, Mrs Brooks, and congratulations on the new baby!'

I said, 'Yes, we are all really looking forward to meeting Dave!' and Mum shot me a warning look.

Next, Toby started demonstrating his armpit-fart skills. He can fart the *Star Wars* tune, which is kind of cool, I guess (if you like that sort of thing).

Then Dad was like, 'Ahhh, the famous Jessica! It's so good to meet you!'

'Hi, Mr Brooks, it's good to meet you too,' said Jess.

'It's Jess!' I said.

'OK, Lottie Potty, whatever you say.'

I rolled my eyes at him. He knows I hate that stupid nickname.

'Sorry. Jess and Lottie – I got it,' Dad said, giving me a wink.

That was when I made the executive decision to get us some privacy in my room.

We got my Sylvanians out from under the bed – they were still there from when I'd shoved them away when Liv came over – and Jess got to work setting up the bakery for me.

'My mum bought me sanitary pads the other day,' I said cautiously. 'In case I . . . you know . . . get IT.'

'Do you think you will?' Jess said. 'I don't think I want to. It sounds kind of gross!'

'I know. I do and I don't. I don't want to be the last one to get it, but I don't think I want to be one of the first either. It sounds like a lot of hassle.'

'My mum said it can give you cramps too. I think I'm happy to wait a while yet.'

'Me too. Hey, do you wear deodorant? I can't really tell if I need to.'

Then we spent about twenty minutes trying to sniff our own armpits, and the more we sniffed the worse we smelt.

After we got bored of smelling our armpits, Jess said, 'I've just had an idea. Do you want to see if we can find Theo on Instagram?'

'YES!'

We managed to track him down, but unfortunately his account was private, so we spent about an hour analysing his tiny thumbnail profile photo and discussing whether or not he'd accept our requests if we followed him.

It was so nice having someone to talk to about all of this weird girl stuff!

TUESDAY 14 SEPTEMBER

On Tuesday mornings I have double science. What a way to start the day!

Our science teacher, Mrs Murphy, announced that we were going to be working on group projects. I immediately started to panic. One of the many problems of being unpopular is that, when you have to get into groups, you always get left with the misfits nobody else wants to work with – AKA me.

Jess is in a different science class, so I put my head down and pretended that I didn't care who I worked with, and then the strangest thing happened. I heard a voice that sounded suspiciously like Amber's say, 'Hey, KitKat girl, you wanna go with us?'

I literally almost fainted! **I MEAN, OMG!**

I tried my hardest to sound super chill and said, 'Sure.'
Then I started moving over to their desk. Unfortunately,
my limbs decided to do something entirely different and
I tripped over absolutely nothing. The contents of my
backpack went flying across the floor. When I looked up,
I wished I hadn't. On the floor, right next to Amber's foot,
lay Mrs Fluffy Bottom! How did she even get there?!

'Errr . . . Why have you got a toy rabbit in your bag?'
said Poppy.

My face burned and I felt the whole class's eyes on me.
'Oh . . .' I said. 'It's my little brother's . . . I have no idea
why he put it in my backpack . . . I hate those dumb
things . . .'

I quickly picked up all my stuff, smoothed out my hair, then sat down in the spare seat at their table. I tried to appear as unfazed as possible. Amber and Poppy both sat there looking really confused for what seemed liked AGES, but eventually Amber broke the awkward silence.

'Hey, I'm Amber, and this is Poppy,' she said. Like I didn't know!

'Hey, I'm Lottie. It'll be nice to be working together.' Why was I talking like an accountant?!

Poppy just smiled and said, 'Cool. KitKat Chunkys are my favourite too.'

Mrs Murphy told the class to be quiet, and started explaining what the group projects were. Each group would be given a different type of force to conduct scientific experiments into, and we'd then have to report our findings to the class. Our group was given gravity. Mrs Murphy said we could use the rest of the lesson to write our objectives and start thinking about our methodology.*

*Fancy word for how you do the experiment.

'So, uh, I guess the objectives should be –' I began.

'Lottie, slow dooooooown!' Amber interrupted. 'Poppy and I usually play Snog Marry Avoid during science, which is obviously MUCH more important than gravity!'

'Well,' I tried to joke, 'without gravity they, uh, the boys, would just float away, so it is actually pretty important . . .' Why am I like this?!

'Look,' Poppy said, 'science is boring! And anyway gravity is super easy! See.' She knocked her pencil case off the table. 'Quelle surprise. It fell to the ground. Experiment done!'

'But,' Amber said, 'if you don't want to be in our group, then . . .'

'I do! Sorry.'

'OK, cool. Sorted. Right, I'll start. Bradley, Leo, Daniel,' Amber said, naming three boys in our science class. 'Snog Marry Avoid? You go first, KitKat Chunky.'

I panicked again.

'Um . . . um . . . um . . .'

'Oh, come on,' said Amber. 'It's not that hard. OK, I'll go first. Snog Bradley, marry Leo and avoid Daniel!'

'Snog Leo, marry Bradley and avoid Daniel!' Poppy chirped confidently.

GULP – now it was my turn. It would have been easier to play if *Theo was there. Snog Theo, marry Theo, avoid everyone who isn't Theo* . . .

Leo and Bradley were at the table behind us. I considered copying the girls' answers, just to be safe, but when I looked round the boys were both picking their noses and comparing boogers. I mean, could you be any grosser? How on earth can Amber and Poppy find *that* attractive?

In comparison, Daniel seemed friendly and – most importantly – clean, so I said, 'I'd snog Daniel and –'

Poppy and Amber burst out laughing before I could finish.

'Daniel! Really?' said Poppy.

And then the worst thing happened.

The whole class spun round and stared at me.

'Girls, quieten down or you are all off to detention!' bellowed Mrs Murphy.

It was so unfair. Poppy and Amber had both said who they wanted to snog and I hadn't announced it to the ENTIRE class! How could they do this to me?

My face burned and I kept my head right down,
pretending to read my text book, until the laughter
eventually died down.

After class, as we were packing up our stuff, Amber said,
'Sorry, Lottie. I didn't mean to shout it out. It was just a
shock, that's all. I mean, Daniel? He's just so geeky!'

I had known I'd get it wrong. That was exactly why I
hadn't wanted to play.

'That's OK,' I said, trying to sound all casual about it.

The funny thing was, though, that as we were filing out
of class Daniel said goodbye to me.

'I think he actually likes you!' said Poppy, giggling.

'Yeh, you'd better set him straight before he gets his hopes up!' added Amber.

WEDNESDAY 15 SEPTEMBER

Had drama today.

I had to pretend to be a cucumber.

Too mortified to write about it right now.

8.43 p.m.

OK. Maybe I'm ready to tell you about it. Maybe writing it down will help. I doubt it, but what else have I got to lose?

So, first, Mrs Lane had us all sit in a circle, then she said, 'Today we are going to cover improvisation. For a warm-up exercise, you are each going to have a turn going into the middle of the circle and acting out something suggested by another student.'

CREEPING DREAD

'As an actor, you will frequently find yourself put on the spot,' she continued. 'That's when you need to improvise! So, let's practise.'

As each person went into the middle of the circle, the other kids would put up their hands and Mrs Lane would pick someone to make the suggestion. There were things like 'zombie', 'mouse' and 'a thunderstorm'. Then all of a sudden it was my turn.

My heart started beating really fast as I tentatively stood up. *Please, someone say something easy!* I silently prayed.

'Would someone like to make a suggestion for Lottie?' asked Mrs Lane.

Amber's hand shot straight up, and I started getting a bad feeling that she wasn't about to make things very easy for me.

Please don't pick Amber . . . pick anyone but Amber . . .

'Amber,' I heard Mrs Lane say.

'I'd like to see Lottie impersonate a cucumber!' she said with a big grin on her face.

I mean, what? What is a cucumber supposed to do? A cucumber is just a cucumber.

So I walked into the middle of the circle and just stood there with my arms by my side, doing nothing.

'Come on, Lottie,' said Mrs Lane. 'Use your imagination. How can you let the audience know that you are a cucumber?'

I felt like crying because I didn't know. Cucumbers don't **DO** anything. That's the point. They just get chopped up to go in a salad!

All I could think to do was to keep standing there, with my arms by my sides, looking as much like a cucumber as possible. Then I said:

Everyone in the room was doubled over in fits of laughter – including Theo!

I mean, what was I thinking? **I TASTE GOOD IN SANDWICHES?** Really?!

Woe is me.

PS Writing it down has not helped.

THURSDAY 16 SEPTEMBER

KitKat Chunky is no more. Everyone is now taking great delight in calling me Cucumber Girl – including Theo. He shouted it out in the corridor this morning.

Jess assured me that he said it in an affectionate way. 'Look on the bright side,' she added. 'At least he knows who you are now.'

I can't say I'm entirely convinced.

THOUGHT OF THE DAY:
Is it better for the boy you fancy to be
A) oblivious to your existence, or
B) reminded of cucumbers every time he sees you? Answers on a postcard please.

FRIDAY 17 SEPTEMBER

Woke up and decided to WhatsApp Molly for advice.

ME: What do you do when everyone thinks you are a cucumber?

MOLLY: I don't know. What do you do when everyone thinks you are a cucumber?

ME: What?!

MOLLY: I don't get it?

ME: Get what?

MOLLY: The joke!

ME: I didn't get this out of my joke book, Molly. THIS IS MY ACTUAL LIFE!! 😬

Then I went down to breakfast and, for some stupid reason, told Dad about my new nickname.

BIG MISTAKE.

Guess what he put in my packed lunch? Yep, you got it. Cucumber sandwiches.

HILARIOUS

SATURDAY 18 SEPTEMBER

Mum said that she is having her baby scan next week and, since Dad is away being all important at work, I can go along if I like. Apparently we will find out whether it's going to be a girl or a boy.

I'm not sure what'd be worse – a mini me or a mini Toby?!

I asked Mum, and she said, 'Well, you're both pretty awful, so I guess it doesn't make much difference!'

Charming.

MONDAY 20 SEPTEMBER

Beautiful Theo walked past me in the corridor today and said, 'Hey, Cucumber Girl. How's things?'

I was a bit flustered and said, 'Errr . . . cool.'

He laughed. 'Cool as a cucumber! I like it. You're pretty funny, Cucumber Girl.'

'Thanks,' I said, even though I was only funny by total accident.

Amber saw the whole thing and looked pretty impressed. 'I can't believe he spoke to you' she said later.

I must admit, nor can I.

TUESDAY 21 SEPTEMBER

Drama tomorrow. What will they make me do this time?! Act out the balcony scene from Romeo and Juliet while pretending to be an aubergine?

WEDNESDAY 22 SEPTEMBER

Drama was fine. We worked on how facial expressions convey emotions, and I did not have to pretend to be an item of agricultural produce. Thank goodness for that.

Theo smiled at me. I think. Maybe he just had the sun in his eyes. I'm going to pretend it was the former.

THURSDAY 23 SEPTEMBER

I went with Mum to her scan today. It was **AMAZING**!

I know I've not been the most overjoyed at the baby news, but I might have been being a *tad* selfish.

Have you ever seen a baby inside someone's tummy on the screen? You can see the teeny-tiny arms and legs and everything. It's bonkers!

And it was so strange because, until I saw that little baby moving around in there, I hadn't really envisaged it as an actual, real, alive person who would be part of our family. Suddenly I felt super excited to meet it.

The lady doing the scan took lots of measurements and said that the baby looked very healthy. Then she said, 'Would you like to know the sex?'

Mum looked at me. 'What do you think, Lottie? Should we find out?'

It was so nice of her to ask me, so I said, 'Yes, I think we should!'

The lady turned to me. 'Well, we can never be one hundred per cent sure, but it looks like you are going to get a little sister.'

A little sister . . . I am getting a little sister! That is so much better than another smelly little brother! Well, hopefully anyway . . . Maybe I could pass my Sylvanian Families on to her to treasure as an heirloom? I wouldn't dream of passing them on to Toby. He'd probably have the entire Fluffy Bottom family massacred by his WWF figurines.

Mum looked really happy at the news too, although I think she was less keen on my new name suggestion.

Ooh, we can call her Davina!

SATURDAY 25 SEPTEMBER

12.35 p.m.

I was feeling bored (as usual), so I was looking at Theo's Instagram profile (as usual). And then a strange gust of confidence came out of nowhere and made my finger hit the follow button!

12.37 p.m.

WHY DID I DO THAT?! WHY? WHY? WHY??!

He is probably laughing at me. He is probably telling all his friends, 'OMG, that weird Cucumber Girl followed me on Instagram. Why doesn't she get a life?'

3.12 p.m.

I am never going back to school again. This is the worst thing that has happened to me. **EVER.** I need to go into hibernation. I wish I was a tortoise.

Can hardly write this, I am hyperventilating so much.
HE HAS ACCEPTED MY FOLLOW REQUEST!

HE HAS REQUESTED TO FOLLOW ME BACK!!!!!!!!!

5.43 p.m.

I HAVE APPROVED HIS FOLLOW REQUEST!

I waited an entire six minutes so as not to look too keen.

#PROUD

5.49 p.m.

HE HAS LIKED ONE OF MY PHOTOS!!!!!!!!!!

I mean, it's a photo of me playing Chubby Bunny, with fourteen marshmallows stuffed in my gob, so I wasn't exactly looking my most attractive, but still!

4 Likes

New record — 14 !!! 🐰👍

10.24 p.m.

Must go to sleep. I have spent four hours looking
through Theo's photos. Some may question whether
that was a bit too long, but I'd say that it was time well
spent. I now know everything from his shoe size (five) to
the brand of toothpaste he uses (Colgate Triple Action in
original mint).

SUNDAY 26 SEPTEMBER

Plot twist.

So Dad was reading the Sunday papers and came across a piece called 'Making Sure Your Child Stays Safe Online', which helpfully informed him that the minimum age for an Instagram account is thirteen! *Grrrrr* at newspapers and their information-sharing!

He went off on one to Mum, and now they are both panicking and saying they need to go through my phone and delete all my 'unsuitable apps'!

I have pleaded my case as well as I can. I have played the pity card. I have assured them that my Instagram is private, and I only use it to share photos with a few close friends – including Molly, my BFF, who has been forcibly removed from my life.

They are going to 'think about it'.

Have now gone to bed, feeling incredibly stressed.

MONDAY 27 SEPTEMBER

Thank the high heavens! The parents have agreed that I can keep Instagram, as long as they can do spot checks on my phone to reassure themselves that I am not up to no good.

I want to know what they think I would be getting up to. The most exciting thing I have done in the last few weeks is to reorganize my bookcase into rainbow colour order.

After dinner, Mum made me show her my followers. Unfortunately, that meant explaining who Theo was, which was . . . interesting.

TUESDAY 28 SEPTEMBER

Jess invited me over to her house after school. I texted Mum, and she said it was fine. Jess only lives a few streets away, so it's mega convenient – almost like it was meant to be!

Jess's parents are divorced, so she just lives with her mum and her little sister, Florence, who is two and a half. Their house is pretty much like ours but, instead of being all white and grey, every room is bright and colourful. It makes you feel happy just being there.

When Jess's mum opened the door, she said, 'Hi, Lottie. I'm Roxanne. Come in, come in! Any friend of Jess's is a friend of mine!' She gave me a huge grin just like Jess had the day she asked me to have lunch with her.

Florence followed us around the whole time I was there. I think she is the cutest kid I have ever met. She doesn't speak a huge amount yet, but she loves cuddles – she kept saying, 'Ottie, uddles!' whenever she wanted me to pick her up for a hug. It made me feel so much better about having my own little sister. Maybe I'll be OK at it after all?

I do draw the line at some things though.

When it was dinner time, Roxanne called us downstairs. Everything smelt amazing, but I'd never eaten Jamaican food before, so I started to panic. What would I do if I didn't like it?! Would they think I was really rude?

Roxanne piled my plate up high with jerk chicken, this thing called 'fried breadfruit' that I'd never heard of before, and rice and peas. 'I hope you're hungry, Lottie!' she said, chuckling.

I must have looked a little nervous, as Jess said, 'Don't worry. My mum is a really good cook!'

Luckily, Jess was not wrong. It. Was. Delicious. In fact, it was so delicious I did something I'd never done before and had another helping.

Me actually asking for seconds?!

I'm not going to tell Mum though, as I don't want her getting any ideas about trying to cook me fancy new dinners at home. It's much safer all round when we eat beige stuff out of the freezer.

#NUGGETSTILLIDIE

SATURDAY 2 OCTOBER

Today me and Jess went clothes shopping for the autumn disco. Even though it's not until next month I needed plenty of time to plan an outfit that would make me look irresistibly cool (or just vaguely all right). I mean it is the *highlight* of my social calendar (or TBH the only thing on my social calendar).

I met Jess on the bus. It was ace to go shopping with an actual friend as opposed to just my mum. Especially as she'd given me a whole £25 to spend – **RESULT!**

Jess and I both wanted to make our money go as far as possible, and this is what we bought:

* Me: Glittery silver top (to wear with my denim skirt), cherry lip balm, body spray, glittery nail varnish, Frazzles and a can of Fanta.

★ Jess: Hawaiian jumpsuit, clear mascara,
   hot-pink nail varnish, bubblegum,
   Chewits and a can of Coke.

We were just about to head back to Jess's to try on our
outfits again when we bumped into Amber and Poppy, of
all people!

'Oh look, it's Cucumber Girl!' Amber said, plonking her
shopping bags down next to us.

'What are you guys up to?' asked Poppy.

'We've just been shopping for outfits for the disco,' I
replied.

'So have we! We're just off to Starbucks now, if you guys
fancy joining us?'

Starbucks! Was everyone drinking coffee these days
except for me?! I'd only recently managed to make the
switch from apple juice to Coke. Maybe, as with everything
else, I'm a late developer in the beverage stakes.

'Sorry, we can't. We're just heading back to my house,' said Jess.

'Ah, shame. OK, never mind,' said Poppy, turning to leave.

I had to act quickly! 'Actually . . . I think we do have time,' I said nervously.

'Cool, let's go!' said Amber.

Jess gave me a look that said, *Why do you want to go for coffee with these people?!* I'm not sure she likes Amber and Poppy that much, but I guess she probably doesn't understand what it's like to be made fun of. I really need to make sure that doesn't happen again.

'It might be fun,' I whispered to her as we walked off, and she seemed to relax a little.

Me and my **three** friends being normal on our way to Starbucks!

When we got to Starbucks, I had no idea what to order. Luckily, Amber and Poppy ordered first, and they seemed pretty clued up. Amber ordered a white-chocolate mocha Frappuccino with extra double cream and peppermint syrup, and Poppy ordered a double-chocolate-chip Frappuccino with mango syrup and cookie-crumble topping.

When it was my turn, I just looked at the board with my mouth open wide.

'Can I help you, miss?' said the guy serving me.

'Yes . . .' I said. 'I'll have a . . . strawberry frappa-whappa-thingaling . . . please.'

He looked very confused. 'Do you mean a strawberries and cream Frappuccino?'

'Yes!' Jess said, laughing. 'Yes, that's exactly what she means.'

It turned out Jess didn't get to make her own order, because the strawberry frappa-whappa-thingaling cost

£3.70 and we had to pool our remaining coins to afford it! I mean, how on earth?! That's like seventy-five per cent of my weekly pocket money!

When we sat down with our drinks, Amber said, 'We come here all the time, don't we, Poppy?'

'We do,' Poppy replied. 'It's our favourite place.'

'I, uh, yes . . . It's one of my favourites too,' I lied, wondering if they could tell that I was actually a Starbucks virgin.

Then I took a sip of my (well, our) Frappuccino, and OMG it was, like, **WOW!**

Heaven in a cup!

I kind of got why they were so expensive. But still – you can get a cheeseburger at McDonald's for a quid!

'So,' said Amber, 'you know Theo, right?'

'Not really,' I replied. 'I mean, I know of him!'

'He's gorgeous, isn't he?' said Amber. 'Have you seen his eyes?'

'Yes, we've seen that he has eyes,' said Jess sarcastically.

'He's the hottest boy in school, don't you think?' said Poppy.

'I guess . . .' I tried to be chill.

'Amber is going to ask him to dance at the disco!' said Poppy. 'Wouldn't they make the cutest couple?'

'They really would,' I said.

Even though I felt a bit jealous, I could also see that Theo and Amber would look great together.

Later on, when me and Jess got back to her house, we went to the kitchen and she poured us both big glasses of apple juice.

'Do you mind that Amber likes Theo too?' she asked, as if she was reading my mind.

'I don't know . . . It's a bit strange,' I said. 'But he would never have been interested in me anyway, so I guess it doesn't matter . . .'

'Why would he not have been interested in you?'

'Um, have you seen me?'

'Yes! I see you, and you are amazing!'

'Thanks.' I smiled. 'I'm not Amber amazing though, am I?'

'No. You are Lottie amazing, and that's even better. Oh and, FYI, Amber is not *that* amazing anyway.'

Just then Roxanne came into the kitchen. She started fixing us sandwiches, which was great as I was really hungry after all that shopping.

'Can I see what you girls bought?' she asked.

'Sure,' I said. But, while we were chatting, Florence had snuck in and had already unpacked our shopping for us – and was right at that moment doing a massive wee all over my **BRAND-NEW** top!

'Oh no! I'm so sorry, Lottie,' said Roxanne. 'We're potty-training her at the minute and – as you have probably gathered – she's a little bit hit-or-miss. Don't worry though. I'll stick it in the wash for you now.'

Jess just stood there trying (unsuccessfully) not to giggle at my horrified face.

The worst thing of all is that Florence still expected to get a chocolate button as a reward for doing the wee!

I guess there are some big downsides to little sisters too.

SUNDAY 3 OCTOBER

Woke up in a bad mood because I was having an amazing dream when I was rudely awakened by my annoying little brother flicking me on the forehead and going, 'LOTTIE, LOTTIE, SHE SMELLS LIKE A POTTY COS SHE'S GOT A STINKY BOTTY AND SHE'S REALLY RATHER SNOTTY!'

It was one of those dreams that you really enjoy and was about a world where strawberry Frappuccinos grew on trees. They were free, so you could have as many as you liked **ALL DAY, EVERY DAY!** It was awesome.

OMG! OMG! OMG!!!!! Guess what?!?!?!???!

I got a text!

> **AMBER:** Hey, Cucumber Girl.*
> Do you fancy having lunch
> with us tomorrow?

> **ME:** I'd love to!

> **AMBER:** Cool. Meet me and Poppy
> by the PE block. We usually sit on
> the grass behind it because it's
> more private. We don't want just
> anyone joining us!

> **ME:** C U there! Can't wait xx

I was totally shocked! They were asking **ME** to hang out
with **THEM?** I had kind of figured that the Starbucks
thing was just a random one-off. Could they actually
want to be friends with me?

*Yep, no one's bored of that yet. ←

I only just thought about Jess. We've been having lunch together every day, and Amber didn't mention inviting her at all . . .

OH GOD, HOW AWFUL AM I?!
WHAT HAVE I DONE??

Just a couple of weeks ago I was worrying that I was totally friendless, and now it almost seems as though I have too many friends. Arghhhh! I'm such an idiot!

4.21 p.m.

Decided to message Amber.

> **ME:** Hey, Amber. Looking forward to lunch tomorrow! Do you mind if I bring Jess? L xx

> **AMBER:** Sure, no worries, babe! A xx

> **ME:** Thanks, babe xx

171

THANK GOD FOR THAT!

Then I messaged Jess straight away.

> **ME:** You'll never guess what!!!

> **JESS:** What?!?!

> **ME:** Amber has invited us to have lunch with her and Poppy tomorrow! 🤩

I didn't hear anything for a few minutes, then all I got was this short reply.

> **JESS:** Oh. Cool.

> **ME:** Is that OK? You don't seem that happy about it?

> **JESS:** It's just that sometimes I think they seem a bit full of themselves, I guess.

> **ME:** Really? Why?!

JESS: At the start of term, they pretty much blanked me when I said hello, and then I overheard them saying my hair looked babyish. And don't you remember how they laughed at you for wearing a bra? And at Mia for having hairy legs? Sometimes they just seem a bit . . . I don't know . . . mean.

ME: I'm sure they were just trying to be funny! Oh come on, Jess! It would be SO great to be better friends with them. I mean, of all the people they could ask to lunch* they picked us!!

JESS: OK. Well if you think it'd be fun then let's do it! Xx

ME: YAY xx

I was so glad Jess came round to the idea.

Amber and Poppy are the coolest girls in Year Seven. No one will laugh at me if they know I'm friends with them!

*I didn't tell her that she wasn't actually invited in the first place, obvs.

MONDAY 4 OCTOBER

So today was **LUNCH DAY** and it was perfect.

We shared our crisps and talked about our favourites.

> ★ **MINE**: Pickled-onion Monster Munch.

> ★ **JESS'S**: Tingly prawn cocktail Skips.

> ★ **AMBER'S**: Crispy bacon Frazzles.

> ★ **POPPY'S**: Salt-and-vinegar Hula Hoops.

I know it might sound boring to some people, but talking about crisps is literally one of my favourite topics. If I was on a TV quiz show, crisps would be my specialist subject.

The other exciting topic of conversation was that Poppy has got a boyfriend! Tom asked her out at break, so they've been together for two hours so far.

'What's it like going out with someone?' I asked.

'Oh well, you don't actually *go* anywhere, exactly,' Poppy said. 'You just sort of say you are going out and tell people you've got a boyfriend or a girlfriend but mostly you just ignore each other.'

That seemed pointless to me, so I just smiled, said 'Wow' and tried to look impressed.

'Yeh, I mean it's OK. I'm not too sure about him yet though. I'm still getting over my last boyfriend, Seb . . . That was really serious.'

'How long were you with Seb?' asked Jess.

'One and a half days,' Poppy said sadly. 'We got to the hand-holding stage and everything, but then he dumped me for a girl called Lucy because she gave him a Wagon Wheel.'

'I'm so sorry, Poppy. That's awful,' I said. I mean, Wagon Wheels aren't even one of my top-five snacks!

'It's his loss!' said Amber. 'Any boy who places more value on a Wagon Wheel than he does on his girlfriend is not worth your time.'

Blimey, that girl is SO wise!

Before we went back to class, me and Amber decided to swap pencil cases, as she was getting a bit sick of her hotdog-shaped one and I was getting a bit sick of my watermelon slice. It kind of felt like we were cementing our friendship. If pencil cases were cement . . . or whatever.

The really good news is that even Jess seemed to be coming round to the idea of us all hanging out together. Amber and Poppy are much more chilled out when it's just the four of us.

WEDNESDAY 6 OCTOBER

Today at lunch Amber said, 'If we are becoming a proper gang, then we totes need a proper gang name!'

'That's an ace idea!' I said.

'Thanks,' she said. Then she cleared her throat and said:

'Oooooooh,' we all said in unison. (Although I imagine she didn't think up such a great name on the spot.)

'I love it,' said Poppy, clapping her hands.

'Me too,' said Jess.

'Come on – let's take our first official photo,' I said, smiling and pulling out my phone.

The selfie came out really well, so I tagged everyone and posted it on Instagram. It was my most-liked pic ever!

37 Likes
The Queens of Seven Green
TQOSG # Girlgang
friends4eva

Suddenly it feels like everything is falling into place and like maybe THE PLAN might be working out after all. Just a few weeks ago I felt totally alone, and now I'm one quarter of the Queens of Seven Green, and we are going to **RULE THE SCHOOL!***

Thought of the Day: If you abbreviate our gang name to TQOSG it is very hard to pronounce. Go on, try it – it actually sounds like you are sneezing!

$$\boxed{6.34 \text{ p.m.}}$$

EXCITING NEWS: The Queens of Seven Green have a new WhatsApp group!

Sadly, our first group chat was a little melancholy. (I learnt that word in English today. It basically means super sad.)

POPPY: It's over with Tom 😩

ME: Oh no, what happened?!

*Or just get through the school year without getting picked on or making total idiots of ourselves. That would be just fine with me too . . .

POPPY: Too devastated to talk about it right now. I'll tell you tomorrow at lunch.

AMBER: Well, whatever happened, he's an absolute idiot!

ME: The biggest idiot in all of Idiotsville.

JESS: The most humungous idiot in the entire idiotic idiotverse!

AMBER: Also, he has dirty fingernails.

ME: You know what they say: a dirty-fingernailed idiot is the worst kind of idiot!

JESS: Who says that?!

ME: Erm . . . not sure . . . me?!

THURSDAY 7 OCTOBER

So it turns out that Kacey from Seven Blue asked Tom
out, and he said yes. Apparently he had *forgotten* he was
going out with Poppy!

I asked if there were any chocolate-based snacks
involved in the break-up, but it turned out that a piece
of bubblegum was the culprit. I mean, imagine being
binned for a singular piece of bubblegum. The poor girl
was distraught.

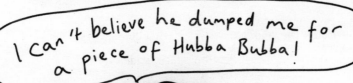

I can't believe he dumped me for a piece of Hubba Bubba!

TBF it was Atomic Apple flavour Hubba Bubba, which is the best, but still . . .

(10.10 p.m.)

Was just about to go to sleep when I got a WhatsApp notification.

MOLLY: Hey, you. I messaged you yesterday and you never replied!

ME: ARGHH, sorry, bestie. I didn't see it pop up. Must have been chatting to the TQOSG.

MOLLY: The who?

ME: The Queens of Seven Green. We have a new gang name! Do you like it?

MOLLY: *Typing . . .*

MOLLY: Oh yes, I saw a pic on Insta of you all. They look like fun.

ME: They are SO much fun!

MOLLY: Cool. Well, glad you've made new friends. Anyway, gotta dash. It's bright and early here, and I'm meeting Isla for a run before school!

ME: A run?!

MOLLY: Yeh, Isla does cross-country for a proper team and everything. I'm going to try and get into it too.

ME: But you hate running!

MOLLY: I guess it just feels different over here because for some reason I'm loving it! Bye x

ME: Bye x

I feel really uneasy now. Things are kind of weird between me and Molly these days. She seems to be spending all her time with this Isla girl . . . and now she's taken up running?! We used to make daft TikTok videos or lie on the sofa eating crisps and chatting. It's like we are living totally different lives. Sometimes I really miss the old days.

FRIDAY 8 OCTOBER

Amber has suggested that now we are an official gang we
should be having regular gang meetings. I volunteered
to have the first meeting at my house, and we all agreed
to meet at 11 a.m. tomorrow morning. Yay! Everyone is
bringing their disco outfits so that we can have a mini
fashion show.

It's so exciting to have MY OWN Saturday plans – ones
that don't involve another trip to Tesco or B&Q with
the parents!

SATURDAY 9 OCTOBER

NERVOUS! Spent the last hour trying to decide which snacks are the right combination of delicious, fun and semi-sophisticated. In the end, I went with Jaffa Cakes, a bowl of mini marshmallows and some of Mum's Waitrose Belgian double-chocolate-chunk all-butter cookies. (Mum will kill me if she finds out, so shhhhhh! Don't tell her!)

3.34 p.m.

Amber and Poppy arrived first, and I introduced them to my mum. Luckily, Dad wasn't there to embarrass me as well, as he had taken Toby to his swimming lesson.

'Hi, Mrs Brooks,' said Amber, looking strangely at Mum's ever-increasing bump.

'Don't worry, girls. I haven't eaten a bowling ball. That is a baby in there,' joked Mum.

'Oh. Errr . . . . weird,' said Poppy.

Mum gave her a funny look.

When Jess arrived, we went up to my room. Amber closed the door quickly and leant against it. 'Oh. My. God,' she said. 'I can't believe your mum is pregnant!'

'Yeh, I know,' I said.

'That means,' said Poppy, looking truly horrified, 'your parents must have been having . . .'

'Yeh, I know,' I said again.

'How old is your mum? Like, forty-two? That is soooooooooooo ancient!' said Amber.

Why does everyone have to keep stating the obvious? I know all this!

'She's forty-one, but whatever,' I replied. 'Who wants to meet my hammies?'

I was very keen to change the subject at this point.

I got the Professor and Fuzzball the 3rd out of their cage and passed them to Poppy.

'Oh my life!' she squealed. 'They are sooooooo cute!'

She and Jess passed the hammies back and forth, letting them run over their hands and down their arms.

Amber looked a bit bored. 'I don't really get hamsters,' she said. 'They seem kind of dumb. I mean, they don't really do anything.'

DUMB?!? What was she even thinking? My hammies are more intelligent than a lot of humans I know! Well, certainly Toby anyway.

'They aren't dumb,' I said as calmly as I could. 'They are actually pretty clever for their size.'

'Really?' said Amber. 'All they do is run round on a wheel for hours on end! Seems pretty dumb to me.'

'Maybe it's time to start our gang meeting,' said Jess.

I picked up the hammies and put them back in their cage, giving them an 'I'm sorry about her' type of look. 'I'll get you some toilet rolls to chew on later to make up for it,' I whispered to them.

The first item on our meeting agenda was Amber's growing crush on Beautiful Theo. (If I'm being totally honest, I still have a Beautiful Theo crush too, but the unwritten rule is that Amber officially dibsed him first.)

'Guys, I **HAVE** to get together with Theo at the autumn disco,' Amber said. 'So we need a plan!'

'Well, what do we know about Theo?' asked Poppy.

'Errr . . . He's Beautiful, he's into football and he's a boy,' Jess offered helpfully.

Not much then.

'You know him best,' said Amber, looking at me. 'Maybe you can help set me up with him?'

'I don't really know him,' I said. 'He just thinks I'm a sandwich filling.'

'Well, that's better than nothing,' she replied.

True.

'So will you help me?'

'I guess so . . .'

Amber clapped her hands, as though this was the greatest idea in the history of the world. 'OMG, you're such a good friend. Thank you sooooo much for doing this for me!'

'Sure!' I replied, trying to swallow the panicky feeling rising in my chest. 'Can't wait!'

I mean, how could I say no?

'Do you like anyone, Jess?' Poppy asked.

'Nah,' Jess replied, casual as anything. 'I'm not interested in boys right now. Eleven is much too young to settle down.'

Amber frowned at her, but you gotta love Jess. She always says it like it is and never tries to impress anyone.

'What about you, Poppy?' I said. 'Do you want to dance with anyone at the disco?'

'No. I'm still getting over Tom, so I think I need to enjoy the single life for a while,' Poppy said. 'Do you know who I think might have a little bit of a crush on you though, Lottie?'

ME? No one has ever had a crush on me before!

'Luis!' she said.

'No way! Ugh,' I said.

'What's wrong with Luis?' said Amber. 'I think he's quite cool!'

'Well, for starters, he has the dirtiest fingernails I ever saw. And have you ever noticed how he always smells of chicken nuggets and potato waffles?'

'It's true!' squealed Jess. 'I'd never thought of it, but now you say it that's exactly what he smells like!'

Everyone laughed a lot, and I felt pretty proud of myself for saying something funny.

Next, we decided to try on our disco outfits. I'd seen Jess's before, but the other girls looked so amazing in theirs. Amber had a mega-classy little black dress, and Poppy was wearing a hot-pink jumpsuit. They both looked a lot older than they are – I'd say at least thirteen and a bit!

Mum shouted up the stairs, 'Can I come and see what you girls look like?'

I said, 'No! It's private!'

The only problem with my outfit was that the top was quite tight. Although I really loved it, it made me look flatter-chested than ever.

'Try putting some socks in your bra,' said Poppy.

'Don't you think you'd be able to tell?' I said.

'I don't know. Give it a go!' said Amber.

So I did, and I admit it did look pretty good (if a little lumpy).

Unfortunately, at that moment Toby decided to burst through my door.

I am seriously considering trying to sell him on eBay.

Actually, scrap that. I'd have to put him on Freecycle. I doubt anyone would actually pay anything for him.

Everyone has gone home now, but all in all I think it was a great first meeting.

Apart from the fact that the responsibility is now on me to help set Amber up with her true love, Theo. There are just two problems with this:

1. I actually quite like Theo too and I can't help feeling a bit jealous.

2. I have the social skills of a turnip. How on earth does Amber expect me to be able to help?

SUNDAY 10 OCTOBER

Mum's a bit peeved.

I got some toilet rolls for the hammies to chew on,
like I promised (can't go back on promises), but Mum
thinks that if there are no used loo rolls in the recycling
then I shouldn't unroll new ones just to get the tubes.
Apparently it's a massive waste and I should think more
about the environment.

Oh no, now she's extra super peeved. Oops.

TUESDAY 12 OCTOBER

It's my birthday in a few weeks' time, and Mum was just asking me what I wanted to do. I hadn't been planning on celebrating it at all, on account of having zero friends, but that's all changed now that I actually have some!

I started thinking of all the things that we could do – bowling, ice-skating, cinema, etc., etc. – but then I figured the funnest thing would be a proper birthday sleepover. I've had Molly stay the night at mine before, but never a whole group of friends. We could order pizza, do face masks, maybe watch a scary movie and really have a proper giggle, just like they do in American movies!

I spent most of the evening designing the invites.

What do you think? Kind of cool, huh!

Can't wait to give them out to the girls tomorrow. ☺

WEDNESDAY 13 OCTOBER

I handed out my invites to Jess, Amber and Poppy as soon as I got to registration this morning. Jess and Poppy looked delighted, but Amber screwed up her nose and said, 'Oh . . . another sleepover party . . . I'll see if I'm free.'

I felt a little bit sad, as I'd spent ages on that invite, but I guess she gets invited to parties all the time and it really isn't that big a deal. I do hope she can come though.

SUNDAY 17 OCTOBER

Just been for a walk round Devil's Dyke. Got halfway
round and Toby suddenly said, 'ARGHHH! I need a poo!'

Mum said, 'Can't you hold it in until we get home?'

He said, 'No, I can't! It's coming right now!'

The upshot is that he had to squat behind a tree and
wipe with leaves. Dad called it a 'wild poo' and said Bear
Grylls would be dead proud.

I was the only one who found Toby exposing his
bottom in public to be rather uncouth, which everyone
found hilarious as, apparently, I used to be quite the
exhibitionist when I was younger.

Mum said, 'Lottie, when you were three years old, you
had a penchant for stripping off naked in the park.
You wouldn't believe how many times I found you

completely starkers apart from a pair of pink wellington boots and had to chase you around the playground. I've got some great photos I'm saving for your wedding day.'

NOTE TO SELF: Never get married.

THURSDAY 21 OCTOBER

A weird thing happened today. Jess was demonstrating her keepy-uppy skills to me in PE, and Theo walked by and said, 'Wow, Jess. You're so good!'

Then he challenged her to a competition. She managed 107, beating her personal best. He only did 35, so she beat him by 79. Call me a maths whizz, huh!

The strange bit was when Amber walked past . . .

She was really off with us for the rest of the day. Maybe she thinks Jess likes Theo, or maybe that Theo likes Jess?!

(EDIT: Jess actually beat Theo by 72. I just checked with a calculator. Oops.)

FRIDAY 22 OCTOBER

I can't believe that today was the last day before half-term. I did it. I made it through.

HERE IS A LITTLE SUMMARY FOR YOU:

* Weeks survived at high school: 7

* New friends: 3

* Times went bright red: 27

* Nicknames: 2

* Crushes: 1

I may still be completely flat-chested, but I have made three friends – and not just that. They are also pretty cool!

THE PLAN actually worked, so I am giving myself a big ol' pat on the back. Well done, me!

The other exciting news is that we now have a week off school and, unlike in the summer holidays, I have people to hang out with. We are planning on shopping, going on the rides on Palace Pier and hanging out in Starbucks a lot. **Hurrah!**

(6.37 p.m.)

I spoke too soon. There is now a massive spanner in the works.

Dad came home from work and said that he had a surprise for us all. Naturally, I was quite suspicious, considering the quality of recent surprises (i.e. Davina).

Mum said, 'What surprise?' in a very unimpressed manner. It seems she was equally suspicious.

Dad said, 'We're going on holiday!'

'YAY!' cried Toby.

I was slightly less excited, seeing my plans to hang out with my mates disappear down the toilet. But then I figured that bathing in the crystal-clear waters of some far-flung corner of the world might take the edge off a bit.

'Oh, darling! That's marvellous!' said Mum, throwing her arms round Dad. 'Where are we going? Italy? Greece? Thailand?'

Dad rubbed his hands together and announced proudly, 'We're going to a caravan park in Wales!'

COMMENCE LONG AWKWARD SILENCE DURING WHICH EVERYONE JUST STANDS THERE, LOOKING HORRIFIED

So Dad's surprise didn't go down particularly well after all.

I mean, no offence to Wales, but it's no Barbados, is it?

Mum seemed to take it the worst. Some particularly colourful language came out of her mouth that I won't repeat here.

7.11 p.m.

In the Queens of Seven Green WhatsApp group:

AMBER: Hey, guys! Fancy going to watch a film on Sunday?

ME: I wish. My dad has booked a surprise holiday to a caravan park in Wales 🙁

AMBER: My condolences.

JESS: Sad times! We will miss you!!!

POPPY: Noooooooooo! Gutted!

ME: Will miss you guys so much too. Don't forget me xxx

JESS: Never xx

SATURDAY 23 OCTOBER

Spent the day packing. Very boring. Thought the frosty atmosphere had improved a bit though.

Then Dad told Mum it was a five-hour drive and we'd have to leave at six in the morning to avoid traffic.

Now she is trying to murder him with a baguette.

I think she has some anger-management issues.

I left the room when I heard Dad saying, 'Calm down, dear!' as that NEVER ends well.

SUNDAY 24 OCTOBER

And we're off, albeit at a later-than-scheduled time,
on account of Dad misplacing the car keys just as we
were about to leave. After two hours of searching, they
eventually turned up at the bottom of the bin, inside an
old tin of tuna. Turned out he'd accidentally chucked
them in there while clearing up the breakfast things.

Oh, we did laugh!

I'm being sarcastic, in case you couldn't tell. A bit of bin
juice never killed anyone though, right?

So now we are on the road. Mum is quietly fuming and
Dad is trying to cheer everyone up by talking about all
the places we'll be able to go and all the things we'll be
able to see when we get to Wales.

I said, 'Doesn't it always rain in Wales though?'

Dad said, 'No, of course it doesn't always rain in Wales! That's an old wives' tale!'

Looked up the weather forecast on my phone: rain every day. Decided to keep it to myself for the time being, as I didn't want to bring the mood in the car down any further. They'll find out for themselves soon enough.

PS Guess what the caravan park is called? Sunny Beach. Oh, the irony!

6.49 p.m.

We've arrived, and who'd have thought it? It's raining!

I loved the sign on the way in, which someone had helpfully customized.

The journey turned out to be more like eight hours, thanks to bad traffic and Mum and Toby's frequent wee breaks. Still, never mind. We are here now and currently settling into our Deluxe Caravan, which is basically a tin shed on wheels. I'd hate to think what the Standard Caravan is like.

For starters, ours is tiny and the decor is awful. Think lots of beige with pink floral furnishings. Dad is trying to call it 'retro chic' but IMO it's more 'Nana's tea party'.

Oh yeh, the whole place also smells of dogs. Apparently Dad left it too late to book and when he did there was only 'pet-friendly' accommodation left. 😬

I don't think Mum's particularly happy about it either, as she's gone 'for a lie-down'. Dad is currently making us beans on toast for tea, and Toby is bouncing about the place declaring, 'THIS IS THE BEST HOLIDAY EVER!'

There is literally no escaping him.

The worst part of it all is that we have to share a room (which is more like a cupboard). I'm writing this perched on my lumpy, narrow bed, and he has just come in and done three farts right next to my actual face.

When I complained, he said, 'I didn't fart on you, Lottie. I just blew you a kiss with my bottom.'

Little brothers are **SO** gross!

MONDAY 25 OCTOBER

Got up and tried to have a shower, but the water would only come out as a tiny trickle. It looks like I'll be stuck with greasy, flat hair for the next week!

Then it started raining and it did not stop **ALL DAY**.

We went to explore the campsite, but there is very little to explore.

There is a minimart, a bar and a death-trap play area that looks like it was built in the 1950s. There isn't even a swimming pool. Mum says it's like a VERY downmarket version of Center Parcs.

I'm not even sure why they bothered making a site map, TBH.

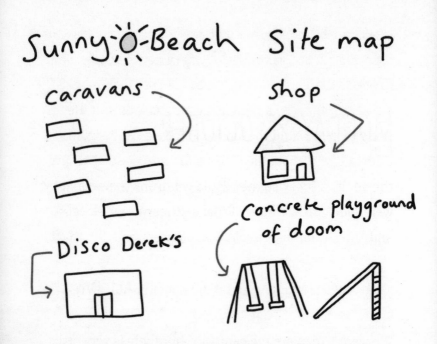

Sunny Beach Site map

Caravans

shop

Disco Derek's

Concrete playground
of doom

Dad said, 'Disco Derek's sounds like it'll be fun, doesn't
it?' and we all just gawped at him.

On account of the terrible weather, we went back to the
tinpot caravan and everyone sat about looking quite
sad – except for Toby, who started playing The Floor
Is Lava and shouting, 'ARGHHH! THE FLOOR IS LAVA!'
every ten seconds at a volume of a hundred decibels. (For
reference, a normal speaking voice is about fifty decibels,
while a boom box is a hundred. I learnt that in science!)

After dinner (more beans on toast), there was a choice of checking out the bar or literally nothing else, so we went to check out the bar. When we arrived at Disco Derek's, we were greeted by a man in a giant penguin suit. He was trying to get all the kids to join 'Pete the Penguin's Club of Fun'. I think the club's main purpose was to give the adults a break so they could get drunk in peace. Toby went, but I flatly refused. What self-respecting eleven-and-three-quarter-year-old would lower herself to that?

TUESDAY 26 OCTOBER

Rained again.

I played 147 games of Connect 4 with Toby and
won approximately 128. Not bad. The ones I lost were,
more than anything else, down to slowly losing the
will to live.

In the evening, we went to Disco Derek's, and . . . Please
don't judge me for what I am about to tell you. The
boredom must have started attacking my brain cells.
OK, here goes . . .

I joined Pete the Penguin's Club of Fun.

The memories of doing the hokey-cokey with a grown
man dressed as a penguin will never leave me.

Going to curl up in a little ball in the dark now. Wake me up when it's time to go home.

PS Please do not breathe a word of this to anyone EVER!

THOUGHT OF THE DAY:
Why do penguins have wings if they can't fly? Do they get jealous of other birds who can fly? I think I'd be pretty annoyed about it if I was a penguin, because flying looks awesome.

WEDNESDAY 27 OCTOBER

(1.34 p.m.)

Yep, you guessed it: still raining.

Sent a postcard to Molly.

S. O. S.
Stranded in a
tin box in wales,
keep getting
accosted by a mad
penguin →
send help!
     Lottie xxx

AFFIX
STAMP
HERE

Molly Lawrence
27 Collins Lane
Sydney
Australia

Tonight was Pete's night off. Thank goodness for that, I thought. Then I heard it was karaoke night, and my heart sank. I looked at Dad and said, 'I hope to the high heavens that no one is thinking about getting up there and embarrassing me.'

Dad said, 'No, of course not, darling. Don't be silly.'

Two pints of lager later . . .

Dad said, 'I mean, I'm not one to boast, but I do a pretty good version of Whitney Houston's "I Wanna Dance With Somebody" . . .'

Mum said, 'Oh, Bill, no. Please don't do this to us.'

I said, 'Dad, I couldn't sleep properly for a week after you did Beyoncé's "Single Ladies" in that bar in Costa Brava in 2018. I'm begging you – stay in your chair!'

But he would not be swayed.

Oh, the shame!

THURSDAY 28 OCTOBER

8.14 a.m.

Oh my word, we have clear blue skies. **WAHOO!** Mum
is currently making sandwiches, and then we are off for
a day at the beach! Apparently there's an arcade and an
amusement park with a fresh doughnut stall. **YAY!**

11.12 a.m.

Started raining after all.

Everything was shut.

Tried to make the best of it.

Then it started hailing.

Toby was delighted.

Everyone else was crying.

Got drenched.

Came back to the tinpot caravan.

Can't feel my fingers.

Or my toes.

Or my nose.

When is it time to go home?

Wow, that almost reads like a really sad poem! May submit it as part of my English poetry module.

#EVERYCLOUD

1.45 p.m.

Things have perked up a bit. Mum got us all towels, and I dried off and put on my comfiest trackie Bs. Then for lunch we had tomato soup and toast by the gas fire and played Monopoly.

I was the old boot (my fave) and I managed to get hotels on Park Lane and Mayfair. I wiped the floor with the lot of them. **HA HA!**

I've always been really excellent at Monopoly. Maybe I'll be a property tycoon when I grow up? Although I'm not entirely sure what that is . . . Perhaps it's a posh estate agent or something?!

7.47 p.m.

Oh lord. We are at Disco Derek's and Pete is back.

Tonight he is holding The Sunny Beach Penguin Olympics.

Sounds pathetic. Totally not doing it.

9.17 p.m.

I won the gold medal in the egg-and-spoon race in the nine- to twelve-year-old category.

I was the only one who entered, but I will not let that small detail dull my shine.

TODAY I AM AN OLYMPIAN!*

*If the Olympics were held at a caravan park in Wales, included only one entrant per category, and were judged by a middle-aged man in a penguin costume.

9.35 p.m.

I was on my way to the toilet when I caught Pete smoking by the fire exit!

He begged me not to tell anyone, and said that Disco Derek would sack him if he found out.

Apparently it took him ages to find this job after he was made redundant three months ago. His previous job was as Kevin the Koala at Crazy Monkeys soft-play centre.

I told him that smoking is very bad for a penguin's health and that it wasn't a good look for an Olympic host either.

'I will ONLY keep your secret,' I said, 'if you promise to try really hard to give up.'

He said he would. He also said that his name wasn't really Pete – that's just his stage name.

Guess what his actual name is?

MARTIN.

I think I preferred Pete . . .

(10.10 p.m.)

Looked on my weather app before I went to bed and apparently there is a storm coming. Joy!

FRIDAY 29 OCTOBER

1.33 a.m.

Awake and huddled in Mum and Dad's room. Sounds like someone is pelting rocks at the caravan.

2.47 a.m.

The caravan is actually rocking. Mum and I are holding on to each other, crying.

3.11 a.m.

I cannot believe Toby and Dad are sleeping through this!

Fairly certain we are about to take flight. I feel like Dorothy in *The Wizard of Oz*. Maybe we'll wake up in Kansas?!

THOUGHT OF THE DAY:
If we all die here and someone finds this diary, please tell Professor Barnaby Squeakington and Fuzzball the 3rd that I love them with all my heart and that I'm sorry for the times I complained about cleaning out their cage. It's just, you know, no one really likes having to deal with poo, do they? Even if they are tiny hamster poos.

Please give my make-up and clothes to Molly, including the denim jacket that she's always liked with the glitter patches on the elbows. Jess can have my Sylvanian Families collection. (I don't mind if she sells any duplicates.)

My Bieber memorabilia can go to charity. Unless a museum would like it? I do have a limited-edition set of coasters and a pair of 'as new' slippers that I only ever wear for five minutes at a time. Very toasty, they are!

Oh . . . sorry about the state of my bedroom. I had meant to tidy it up, but I'm a busy pre-teen. You know how it is.

IMPORTANT: DO NOT LET THIS DIARY GET INTO THE HANDS OF ANYONE AT KINGSWOOD HIGH. IDEALLY YOU WILL BURN IT IMMEDIATELY. (In a safe and controlled manner, obvs. I don't want any more lives to be needlessly lost.)

Do you want the good news or the bad news?

The good news is that I'm not dead. Yay!

The bad news is that, although the storm has now passed, it's taken with it the camp's electricity and heating.

Dad just got up, did a big yawn and said, 'Morning, campers! Did everybody have a good sleep?'

If looks could kill, Dad would have died a thousand times.

Mum said, 'I'd like to go home now please, Bill,' but in slightly ruder language.

SATURDAY 30 OCTOBER

Hurrah! We are finally home!

Mum said there were to be no more holiday surprises. Particularly not ones involving caravan parks in Wales in October. She says that next time she is going to an all-inclusive resort in the Seychelles. Alone.

Poor old, deluded Mum. I think she has forgotten about being pregnant with Davina.

SUNDAY 31 OCTOBER

Happy Halloween!

Not that I care. I'm way too old for that whole trick-or-treating shizzle these days.*

Mum annoyingly made me take Toby up and down the street, on account of her being too tired from all the baby-growing and Dad being too tired from the long drive. Both problems of their own making, if you ask me but as they frequently tell me, 'mine is not to reason why'.

I asked Toby what he wanted to dress up as. A skeleton? A devil. A ghost?

*Will obviously be helping Toby eat his haul though. It was a good one this year. Lots of mini Mars bars. Yum.

Guess what he picked?

A banana.

I said, 'Toby, I really don't think there is anything very scary about a banana.'

'What if I start growling?' he said.

'Have you ever heard a banana growl?'

'Er, no.'

'That's because they are generally pretty silent.'

'What if I carry an axe?' he said.

'Yeh, that could work, I guess.'

So that's the story of how I went trick-or-treating with an axe-wielding, growling banana.

$\longrightarrow$

PS Mum forgot to get sweets, so our house got egged.
Proper LOLs.

7.27 p.m.

Just remembered I haven't done any of my homework.

Oh well. Just two essays, a maths paper and a still-life
drawing to complete before tomorrow.

Right, I'm hunkering down.

IT WILL BE FINE.

Won't it?

8.17 p.m.

Why oh why aren't my hammies any good at equations?!

10.26 p.m.

So tired. Having a bowl of Rice Krispies for energy. Still have my art to do. Is a still life of a bowl of Rice Krispies OK, do you think?

Mum's just woken me up. I'd fallen asleep at my desk,
face first in my cereal bowl. I was having a nightmare
that I was flailing about in the sea, getting chased by a
family of great white sharks.

When I woke up, I was still trying to fight them off with my
spoon (which I doubt would have been very effective in a
real shark-attack scenario). It was all very disorientating.

In the commotion, my still-life drawing got milk all over
it, so now it is ruined and it is too late to start again. I
will have to say the hammies ate it.

MONDAY 1 NOVEMBER

Woke up at 8.23 a.m. and panicked. I chucked my
uniform on and ran out of the door.

When I got to registration, I gave Jess, Amber and Poppy
big hugs. It was so lovely to see them all again – that was
until Poppy gave me a funny look and said really loudly
(as in, so loudly that the entire class stopped talking and
looked at me), 'Lottie, what is that in your hair?'

I put my hand up to feel where she was pointing, and
a bunch of Rice Krispies fell out of my ponytail. I must
have been so exhausted last night that I flopped into bed
without properly de-Krispie-ing myself, and I hadn't had
time to brush my hair or even look in the mirror before
leaving the house this morning.

How disgusting am I?!

By lunchtime all of Year Seven had heard the hilarious tale of how I came to school with a barnet full of breakfast cereal. Can you guess what my new nickname is?

Yep. You got it . . .

That's her! That's Rice Krispie head!

Brilliant.

At lunchtime we talked about our half-terms, and everyone else's sounded infinitely more exciting than mine. Amber and Poppy had seen each other practically every day, but Jess hadn't hung out with them. I thought that was a bit odd.

When Jess and I were alone together in English class, I said to her, 'How come you didn't end up seeing the girls over half-term?'

'I don't know . . .' she replied. 'I didn't hear from them much, I guess. But no worries. I was really busy anyway. Me, Mum and Florence made loads of plans!'

She did look a little bit sad about it though.

WEDNESDAY 3 NOVEMBER

Since it's my birthday on Saturday and the school disco is next Friday, I was wondering if I could convince Mum and Dad to let me get my hair balayaged like Liv's.

Dad's usually the weakest link, so I waited until he was at his happiest (sitting down in his slippers, reading the paper), then I said dead casually, 'Dad, I was thinking . . . You know, I've been **REALLY** good and **SUPER** helpful lately, right?'

'Um . . . Not quite sure that's the case.'

'Well, whatever. Anyway, I was wondering . . . would you pay for me to get my hair balayaged?'

'To get your hair balay-what?'

'Balayaged, Dad. It's French. It's a hair-dying technique.'

'Never heard of it. How much does this balay-whatsit cost then?'

'Oh, you know, it's pretty cheap. Just about –' I may have mumbled the next bit – 'a hundred pounds.'

'ONE HUNDRED POUNDS? You have got to be having a laugh! My haircut costs me six quid!'

'That's because you don't have any hair, Dad!'

'Don't be cheeky, young lady.'

Ugh, parents! Who'd have 'em?!

Later on, just as I was saying goodnight, he came into the lounge to tell me that he had found the perfect solution. It would apparently save **LOADS** of money, as I'd never have to get my hair cut again.

FRIDAY 5 NOVEMBER

Bonfire Night, and my last day as an eleven-year-old.

Dad bought a massive rocket that cost £89. Mum says spending £89 on something you are going to blow up is just burning money. Literally.

I have to admit that I agree. The rocket was pretty impressive, but it only lasted about ninety seconds. Also, I could have got my hair done for that price! (Almost.)

Mum did make the most amazing homemade toffee apples though. They were super sweet and chewy. Delicious! An added bonus was that it took Toby so long to eat his that we had a whole forty-five minutes free from fart jokes or getting karate-kicked in the bum. Pure bliss.

SATURDAY 6 NOVEMBER
(AKA MY TWELFTH BIRTHDAY!!!!!!!!!!!!!)

(10.15 a.m.)

Woke up at 8 a.m. and, before I went downstairs to open my presents, I put on my underwear and had a good look at myself in the mirror. I looked the same, yet also sort of different. Does that make any sense?

My chest is still as flat as a pancake, but at least I don't have spots and my hair isn't so greasy it needs washing every day (yet).

I think my face is looking a little less round though. I wonder what age you start getting wrinkles? Maybe I should start using some of Mum's face cream?

Some days I still feel like a kid.

Other days I feel like I'm growing up too fast, and I want to press the pause button.

In one year I'll be a teenager, so I'm stuck in this strange in-between-y bit for a little longer yet . . . May as well make the most of it!

I pulled on my jeans and a blue-and-white stripy T-shirt, then headed downstairs to find Mum, Dad and Toby in the kitchen. Above them hung two big silver helium balloons saying '21'.

'Um, I think you've aged me nine years!' I said.

They laughed and shuffled the balloons around, then cheered, 'Happy birthday, Lottie!'

Then Mum said, 'I can't believe my baby is so big!' and started full on bawling her eyes out. She always gets overly emotional on our birthdays, and I guess the pregnancy hormones weren't helping things much either.

Dad wasn't much better. 'I can't believe little Lottie Potty is twelve! I still remember the day you did explosive diarrhoea all down my suit, right as I was about to leave for an important meeting.'

'Daaaaaad,' I said, and he gave me a wink and ruffled my hair.

Next, I opened my presents. I had mostly asked for cash to spend on clothes, but I also got a new dressing gown, some body spray, a bubblegum-scented candle, a twenty-four-pack of coloured Sharpies and a melon-and-lime peel-off face mask. **ACE!**

Then we had French toast with strawberries, syrup and whipped cream for breakfast – my favourite.

Now I'm counting down the minutes until 5 p.m., when the girls will arrive for my first-ever birthday sleepover party. **WAHOO!!!!!!!!!!!**

3.17 p.m.

I've not heard anything from Molly. It's really strange. We used to always spend our birthdays together, and now she's not even sent me a WhatsApp, let alone a card or a present?! Could my best friend really have totally forgotten my birthday?

Trying not to let it get to me though. The girls will be here soon, and I still have loads to get ready!

SUNDAY 7 NOVEMBER

Well, I don't want to sound arrogant, but I think
that was the best sleepover party in the history of
ALL SLEEPOVER PARTIES EVER. I mean, Mum
and Dad may have a different opinion, but they weren't
actually invited, so who cares!

First, we set up camp. My room is a little small to fit us
all in, so we took over the lounge. I got the girls to bring
duvets and pillows, and we made one huge bed on the
floor. It was like a giant fluffy marshmallow.

Then Mum let us order pizza for dinner. We got a mega-
deluxe deal with stuffed-crust pepperoni pizza, garlic
bread, chicken strips, double-chocolate fudge-brownie
ice-cream, and one bottle of Fanta and one of Coke.

When we finished eating, I suggested we try my new
peel-off face mask. It was really fun. I squeezed a dollop

into each girl's hands, then we rubbed it all over our faces. It was pretty slimy and felt a bit strange, but after ten minutes it had set and it was like our faces had frozen. My skin felt so tight that I couldn't even speak properly.

I gripped a bit by my cheek, and it started to come off in a sheet.

'Arghhhh, it looks like you are peeling the skin off your face!' cried Poppy.

'She's right! You look like a zombie!' squealed Jess.

We all agreed that it did make your skin feel super fresh and clean afterwards though, so maybe I'll do it every week from now on to keep my youthful appearance.

Next, we got into our jammies and watched a scary movie about a village controlled by a vampire. Every month, the villagers had to sacrifice one of their own to the vampire, or else he would kill the entire town. Everyone who lived there was given a number, and they chose the person who would get sacrificed via a lottery draw. It was like a really horrible version of the tombola you get at school fairs – instead of winning a bottle of bubble bath or a tin of biscuits, you got to die!

The film finished at about 11.30 p.m., and Mum came in and said, 'Right, girls. I think it's time you settled down for the night!'

I don't know where she got the idea that we'd be asleep before midnight. **HA!** Anyway, we were all too scared from the movie to sleep. Poppy asked if she could go home, but Mum looked a bit annoyed and said it was far too late.

To distract ourselves from thoughts of vampires sucking our blood, we decided to raid the kitchen cupboards and eat all the snacks in the entire house! We got an excellent haul, because Mum eats a lot at the minute to help with her morning sickness.

'What does it feel like being twelve?' asked Jess, as we were stuffing our faces with Jelly Babies.

'I don't know . . .' I said. 'I guess it feels kind of the same, but sort of different.'

Suddenly I realized I was officially the oldest one in the room, and I felt quite mature.

'I don't think you start feeling properly grown-up till you have your period,' said Amber.

'You have your period?' I said.

'Yeh, I've had it for *ages*.'

'Ages?!'

'Well . . . a few months. My mum was an early developer too, so I guess it runs in the family.'

'What's it like?' said Jess.

'It's OK. A bit annoying. A bit crampy. It's hard to explain, but you'll understand when it happens to you.' Then she narrowed her eyes and looked at me. 'It's funny how you're the oldest, Lottie, but you don't even have your period yet. And you've got the smallest boobs out of *eeeeeeveryone*. I bet you've never kissed a boy either.'

All eyes turned to me.

I guess I may be the oldest in terms of age, but I always feel so much younger than Amber. She is practically a proper woman. I can't help feeling a tiny bit jealous of how experienced she seems to be about everything.

'I . . . I . . . well . . .' I stammered.

'I've never kissed a boy!' said Jess. 'I don't even want to. It looks gross.'

I gave her a big smile for rescuing me – again.

'Well, you wouldn't know what you're talking about then,' said Amber.

'How many boys have you kissed?' I asked.

Hard to keep count but I reckon about 13 or so!

'Thirteen?!' I cried. 'How have you managed to kiss THIRTEEN boys already? You're only eleven!'

Poppy rolled her eyes and started laughing.

'It's actually true!' said Amber. 'I was on holiday at a campsite in the south of France. French boys are so much more sophisticated than the boys over here.'

'But what she didn't mention is that she was nine years old and it was a game of kiss chase that she kept losing accidentally on purpose.' Poppy giggled.

Amber grabbed a pillow and hit Poppy over the head with it. I don't think she much liked being rumbled, but we all felt much better after hearing that.

I'm quickly learning that you have to take most things that come out of Amber's mouth 'with a pinch of salt', as my dad would say.

I picked up my pillow and started bashing Jess with it, and next thing you know we were having a full-on pillow fight!

The noise must have woken Dad, as he appeared in the doorway looking a bit like one of the vampire's victims and complaining about how late it was.

I said, 'Dad, listen. I know it's late-ish, but we've just eaten a two-hundred-gram bar of Dairy Milk, a multi-pack of Twix, and two and a half bags of Haribo. I don't honestly think we'll be able to sleep for at least a few hours yet.'

Dad looked terrified and left.

I don't know what he was complaining about though. If you're going to leave a bunch of pre-teens with unrestricted access to sugar and gory Netflix movies, what do you expect?!

The next couple of hours were a bit of a blur. We practised headstands, had a dance-off and tried stuffing our bras with marshmallows. (FYI, they work much better than socks AND you can eat them afterwards. Feels a bit sticky though.)

Anyway, everybody else has passed out now, and writing this is making me feel pretty sleepy, so I'd better say nunight and get some shut-eye myself. I did make it to 4.26 a.m., which is pretty impressive for a just-turned-twelve-year-old. Go, me!

(5.46 a.m.)

Oh dear God. I forgot Toby gets up at the crack of dawn.

He's now bouncing in the middle of our marshmallow bed, watching *The Lego Movie* and singing at the top of his lungs.

I have only had approximately forty-five minutes' sleep.

If I had the energy to move my legs, I would kick him.

11.13 a.m.

Everyone has gone. Mum apologized profusely to everyone's parents for the lack of sleep, the sugar intake and the access to violent horror films. *Tsk, tsk.*

I feel incredibly ill. Keep doing fizzy burps that taste of Tangfastics. Kind of gross, but they smell pretty good.

I never thought I'd say this, but I think I'm actually craving some vegetables?!

Dad is looking incredibly smug and keeps going, 'Ahhhhh, poor Lottie Potty. Bit tired, are we? Did you not sleep well last night?'

HILARIOUS.

Message from Molly:

> Molly: OMG I'M SO SORRY I FORGOT YOUR
> BIRTHDAY! I was out training with Isla all
> day and then fell asleep after our mega run.
> Did you have a good party? Please forgive
> me!! xxxx

So she was with Isla. Well, that figures. She's always with Isla. And apparently Isla and her running club are much more important than her BFF turning twelve.

I turned my phone off. Too tired to deal with this right now.

2.47 p.m.

Tried to nap on the sofa, then suddenly Dad was there, using a cordless drill right next to my head. Mum's been on at him for ages to put some shelves up, and today was the day he finally got around to doing it . . .

Personally, I think everyone is taking far too much delight in my suffering.

Not looking forward to school tomorrow. Was all worth it though!

MONDAY 8 NOVEMBER

Feel like the living dead. Everything is such hard work. Going straight to bed when I get home.

Fell asleep three times in science. Mrs Murphy was not impressed. She kept saying, 'Wake up, Lottie. How can you not find igneous rock formation fascinating?'

I was too tired to dignify that with a response, so I just stared at her.

By lunchtime I needed a sugar fix so badly that I downed three slushies to try and wake myself back up. Did I tell you my school canteen does slushies?! You just scan your thumbprint to get one. They're basically free!

Anyway, it worked a treat. After three blue-raspberry-and-watermelon mixes, I was absolutely buzzing!

Came home to a beautiful bunch of flowers from Molly.
I've never had a bunch of flowers delivered to me before.
It felt very grown-up.

I still feel quite hurt though, so I don't know what to
think. I'll message her later.

Right now I have a date with my bed.

TUESDAY 9 NOVEMBER

Slept for fourteen hours last night and felt like a new girl in the morning!

All in all, a much better day.

Apart from the revelation that slushies aren't really free after all. Turns out your parents have to load money on to your virtual account via an app, which also tells them exactly how much you have spent and – crucially – what you have been buying.

It's a bit like spyware and, IMO, ludicrously unfair. (Cool, that rhymes!)

Mum said I should be using my credit to buy myself 'a nice piece of fruit'.

I said, 'Fruit? No one eats fruit when they are hungry!'

She said, 'Of course they do. A banana is a great snack!'

I said, 'I'll remind you of that next time I see you working your way through an entire pack of Jaffa Cakes.'

She didn't really have a comeback to that, so I think I won!

THOUGHT OF THE DAY:
Is a Jaffa Cake actually a cake or a biscuit? I mean, it's called a cake but it looks like a biscuit. V confusing.

TUESDAY 16 NOVEMBER

Amber wants me to introduce her to Beautiful Theo in drama tomorrow. She seems to be under the impression that he and I are actual friends because we're Instagram friends, but they are completely different things. The reality is, I don't think Theo even knows my actual name.

PS Today Poppy told us that her next-door neighbour's cousin's friend's swimming teacher's daughter didn't start her period until she was twenty-nine! What if that happens to me?!?

WEDNESDAY 17 NOVEMBER

Why am I such a social misfit?!

Yesterday in drama, Amber nudged me and said, 'DO IT NOW!'

Try and speak normally, I kept telling myself.

OMG, I JUST NEARLY CALLED HIM BEAUTIFUL THEO TO HIS ACTUAL FACE!

'I meant. I mean . . . Hi, Theo. I said "Theo" because that's your name, isn't it? You're called Theo, right?!'

Please, someone hit the mute button. I need muting urgently!

'Yep, I'm Theo,' he said, 'and you're Cucumber Girl, right?'

'Yeh. Well . . . it's actually Lottie . . . if you like. BUT I do also answer to KitKat Chunky, Cucumber Girl and Rice Krispie Head. Ha ha. Anyway, ah . . . hi.' *You already said that, MORON!* 'This is my . . . ah . . . friend Amber . . .'

Amber shot me a 'what the hell is wrong with you?' type of look, then took over the conversation, as calm as anything.

'Hi, Theo,' she said. 'Nice to meet you. Are you going to the disco on Friday?'

Oh, how amazing it must be to be able to string a sentence together.

'Hi,' he replied. 'Yeh, I guess so.'

'Great! See you there!'

'Cool. See you there or whatever,' he said, then turned back to his friends and started talking about football results again.

I mean, personally, I didn't think the conversation went *that* well, but Amber seemed absolutely delighted.

I do have to agree that they would make a perfect-looking couple though. If this was the United States, they'd be prom king and queen for sure.

THURSDAY 18 NOVEMBER

ONE SLEEP TO GO!

Feeling kind of nervous but in a good way. Tried on my outfit six different times – not sure I've got it completely right but not much I can do about it now, is there?

Thought about texting a picture to Molly to get her opinion, but I can't help still feeling a bit mad at her.

No time to think about that now though – I need my beauty sleep for tomorrow.

Nunight xx

FRIDAY 19 NOVEMBER

DISCO DAY!

My hair has been a bit of a disaster. I tried following a
video tutorial on how to get 'loose, effortless waves' with
a curling wand, but it didn't really work out.

This is
not how
it looked
on
YouTube
⟶

I had to wash it again, then only had time to do it in the
exact same style as usual. Mum said I could wear a little
bit of make-up, so I've got tinted lip gloss, mascara and a
bit of blusher on. I think I look OK.

I decided to ditch the socks-in-my-bra idea and just rock the flat-chested look. I did a little fashion show for the hammies, and they seemed to approve at least!

Just got a WhatsApp notification.

MOLLY: Hey, Lottie. I miss you! It's been ages. Have you got time to chat if I give you a call? xx

ME: Sorry, not now. I'm just off to Amber's for pizza before the disco! Poppy and Jess are coming too. We've all got new outfits and it's going to be so much fun!

> **MOLLY:** OK then. Maybe later. Have a great night. And I'm sorry again that I forgot your birthday x

> **ME:** Don't worry. It was the best birthday ever. I didn't even notice.

> **MOLLY:** Glad you had a nice time.

> **ME:** I did. Oh, and I kept meaning to say thanks for the roses x

> **MOLLY:** No worries x

I might have sounded a little bit blunt, but I'll chat with her tomorrow. Right now I'm **DEAD** excited.

I wonder if Amber and Theo will get together?

I wonder if anyone will ask me to dance?

I wonder if they'll play any Justin Bieber songs and I'll have to pretend to hate it?

I have a feeling that tonight is going to be amazing, and
THE PLAN might finally be coming together. Cinders
is going to the ball and maybe she won't turn into a
pumpkin!

Will report back later . . .

9.49 p.m.

Wow. Well, that was eventful . . . in a bad way.

I don't have the energy to write much right now, so I'll
give you the main points.

FIRST, THE GOOD THINGS (NOTE THIS IS PRETTY SHORT):

* They played 'Sorry' by Justin Bieber.
  (See also: bad points list)

* A boy actually asked me to dance.
  (See also: bad points list)

* Errr . . . that's it.

NOW THE (LONGER) BAD THINGS LIST:

* They played 'Sorry' by Justin Bieber, but apparently everybody was too cool to dance to it. Sad times.

* I was feeling very nervous, so I drank three cans of fizzy drink (two Fantas and one Coke), then had to spend the rest of the evening concentrating super hard on not burping in anyone's face. At one point I felt so full of gas I was worried I might float away.

Everyone else being all normal

Me. About to take off.

* Theo spent all night messing about with his friends, and Amber started getting really annoyed that he hadn't asked her to dance. Then Jess said she was bored of standing on the edge of the dance floor chatting and asked if I wanted to dance. I wasn't sure what to do, so I said I'd better stay with Amber and Poppy. So Jess went over and joined in with the boys!

* Then the three of us stood there watching Jess have loads of fun without a care in the world. Amber was totally furious, and I must admit I felt kind of bummed out too. I like Theo, and Jess knows that . . . Just because nothing will ever happen between us, doesn't mean it didn't hurt to see Jess hanging out with him.

* Five minutes later Daniel came over and asked ME to dance. (I know!) Unfortunately, due to my gas issues and

my problems forming proper sentences,
I just stood there like this:

* Amber butted in and said, 'No, she
  doesn't! Why would she want to dance
  with you?!' and Daniel said, 'OK, no
  worries,' and walked off, looking really
  sad. Then I felt even more rubbish. ☹

* Next, Amber ran off crying, and Poppy
  and I had to spend forty-five minutes

consoling her in a toilet cubicle. We missed the rest of the disco.

* Apparently Amber's heart is broken and she will NEVER recover from Theo's rejection.

* Poppy said Jess was 'all over Theo' (even though I swear they never touched) and 'a really bad example of feminism' (whatever that meant – I'm not quite sure).

* Amber said, 'I can't believe it. Even Lottie got asked to dance!' The 'even Lottie' bit hurt quite a lot. Do they all think I'm pathetic too? I'm trying not to think about that too deeply right now.

* As we were leaving, Amber shouted, 'YOU SELFISH COW!' at Jess. I think she forgot that Poppy's mum was picking us all up and dropping us home.

* In summary, my friends all hate each other and everything is ruined! 🙁

SATURDAY 20 NOVEMBER

A notification popped up on the Queens of Seven Green WhatsApp group:

> **Amber has left the group.**

Mic drop moment!

I mean, talk about brutal.

7.33 a.m.

> **JESS:** What's going on?! All I did was dance and have fun, which is what you are meant to do at a disco, isn't it?!

ME: I know, but Amber thinks you purposely danced with Theo when you know that she likes him . . .

JESS: That's crazy! I don't like Theo like that. We are just friends! You know that girls and boys can be mates, right??

ME: Of course. It's just a silly mix-up. Sure we can sort it all out! x

7.35 a.m.

Message from Amber:

I CANNOT BELIEVE WHAT HAPPENED. MY HEART IS SHATTERED INTO A MILLION PIECES! WHY WOULD JESS DO THAT TO ME? WHY?!??!?!! 😫😫😫

Okaaaaaaay then. Perhaps this isn't going to be quite so easy to sort out after all.

I replied to Jess.

> **ME:** Um, maybe she's a little bit more upset than I thought. She said her heart is broken 🙁 So maybe it might help if you said sorry?

> **JESS:** She needs to get a grip. She's eleven years old, and they aren't married! I have nothing to apologize for!

Next, I replied to Amber. I tried to keep it cheery.

> **ME:** Morning, Amber! Crazy night last night, huh?! Ha ha. Anyway, just to let you know, Jess says she doesn't like Theo at all. So I think it's just been a bit of a mix-up. Phew!

AMBER: WERE YOU EVEN THERE?! She completely hogged him ALL NIGHT! She knew I liked him, and if she was a proper friend then she would NEVER have done that to me! 😣

ME: She said she just wanted to have a dance. I'm sure if she'd known you were upset, then she would have backed off a bit . . .

AMBER: FRIES BEFORE GUYS!

ME: Were they selling fries?! I'd have defo got some if I'd seen them. I was starving!

AMBER: No. It's just a saying, you doofus. Have you never heard of GIRL CODE?!

ME: Oh, yes. Girl Code. Of course I have. But what I mean is, I'm sure it's just a bit of a misunderstanding and we can sort it all out!

When I got up, Mum asked if anything was going on.

I tried my best to explain the situation to her.

'So, Amber likes Theo. Well, we all like Theo, but Amber likes him the most, and Jess and Theo are friends, and I'm sort of friends with Theo, but not really – more like Instagram friends once removed. Anyway, me, Jess, Amber and Poppy were waiting for Theo to ask Amber to dance, and Poppy was going to ask him, but then Jess wanted to dance so she started dancing, and then Theo started dancing with her, but only in a crazy sort of way – not romantic or anything – but Amber didn't see it like that, and she started crying and ran off to the toilets. So Poppy and I had to go and console her, and we spent, like, an hour in a toilet cubicle and used up a whole loo roll, and then the disco was over, and Jess was all like, "Where did you guys go? You missed all the fun!" and Amber screamed in her face, and we all had to get a lift back in Poppy's mum's car, and it was all super weird, and now no one is speaking to each other!'

'Wow,' said Mum. 'Well, I guess you have a very hectic social life these days, Lottie.' She was smiling. 'It does sound like a lot of fuss over nothing though. And it's certainly not worth losing friends over.'

'I know, Mum. Don't worry, I'm going to be the mature one and sort it all out tomorrow.'

'Glad to hear it. Oh, by the way, you need to call Molly back. She phoned yesterday and she sounded rather keen to chat to you.'

'I know. I just haven't had time yet. But I will soon.'

'Good girl. Tell Amber what my mum used to say to me: there are plenty more fish in the sea!'

What a weird thing to say! What does the number of fish in the sea have to do with what we were talking about?!

Plus, if anything, Mum is wrong. We were talking about the consequences of overfishing in geography the other day, and it seriously endangers the ocean's ecosystems!

Weirdly, I keep thinking about Daniel and how nice it felt to be asked to dance.

I wonder what would have happened if Amber hadn't told him no? I guess she was just trying to look out for me . . . but I don't see what would be so wrong about dancing with him? I mean, it's just dancing.

In some ways, I think he's kind of cute . . . or maybe I don't . . .

Oh, I don't know what I think!

I suppose it doesn't matter much anyway, now that he thinks I'm a mute, gassy lemon.

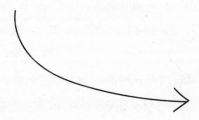

Oh crikey. Amber has uploaded a sad-face cryptic Instagram post.

You think you are friends
- then they stab you in the back.
#heartbroken #betrayed
#crying #whyme #Sad

27 likes

🌹 Babe?! Are you ok?
😭 oh hun. Love ya!
🌹 Sent you a DM babe Xx

THOUGHT OF THE DAY:
If I actually had to choose between fries and guys, it'd be fries EVERY time. I mean, it's not even really a proper choice, is it? Love me a good chip butty!

SUNDAY 21 NOVEMBER

Mum is pretty cross with me, as I've apparently spent nearly all weekend 'staring at my phone'. And, to top it off, she is nagging me about phoning Molly back.

I tried to explain to Mum that I was in full-on crisis-management mode, but she didn't seem to fully appreciate just how dramatic the events of a Year Seven disco can really be.

I've had a funny, churning feeling in my tummy all weekend. I'm really not looking forward to going back to school. Jess doesn't seem to understand what she's done wrong, Amber thinks Jess has committed the crime of the century, Poppy thinks whatever Amber thinks – and me? Well, I guess I'm just stuck somewhere in the middle.

Oh well. Maybe everyone will have forgotten about it by tomorrow?

MONDAY 22 NOVEMBER

Everyone has **NOT** forgotten about it.

I bumped into Amber in the corridor, and I've never seen her look so awful. (Well, I mean awful for Amber – she still looked, like, a billion times better than I ever do.) Her eyes were all red from crying, and she had dark shadows under her eyes.

'I know I look terrible,' she said, 'but this is what happens when you lose someone you love.'

I couldn't believe my ears. 'OH MY GOD! IS THEO DEAD?'

'No, Lottie! Sometimes you really are incredibly dumb. Theo did not die at the Year Seven autumn disco, or not as far as I know,' she said, raising a small smile.

I felt quite insulted TBH, but at least I had cheered Amber up a little bit.

When we got to registration, the atmosphere was icy.
Amber was as frozen as a fish finger that got lost at
the back of the freezer drawer two years ago. Jess was
slightly more approachable, yet still a pretty cross potato
waffle. Poppy and I were just a couple of random peas,
warily observing.

You could have cut the atmosphere with a knife.

And I was the only one who knew where the defrost
button was. So, although it went against everything I am
(I'm more of a take-the-back-seat kinda chick, ya know),

I did what I needed to do: I passed a note round to the girls, asking them to meet by the tuck shop at break.

Then I put on my big girl pants and **I WOMANED UP**!

Determined face →

Big girl pants →

ROAR

Luckily, the girls all turned up.

For about thirty seconds no one said anything, and then everyone started talking at once.

'WHOA! WHOA! WHOA!' I said. 'Let me speak first.'

I'd prepared a little bit of a speech in my head. It was the kind of thing that seemed to work well in films, so I went with it.

'I just think this has all been a bit of a misunderstanding, guys. Jess just wanted to dance and didn't realize that Theo was in such close proximity! She didn't know that Amber was upset, and if she *had* known then she would have spent all night in the toilet too. Right, Jess?'

Jess looked a bit unsure about this, but I nodded at her reassuringly.

'Ummm . . .' she said.

'Great! And Amber had been looking forward to dancing with Theo for two whole days, so she was understandably completely devastated and angry at Jess, because she felt like Jess was trying to sabotage her plan. Isn't that right, Amber?'

'YES! And she knew that, and she still did it!' She pointed angrily at Jess.

'BUT,' I said, 'Jess understands that now, and I think it would be the Christian thing to forgive her. I think it's what Jesus would have wanted.'

Not sure why I started going on about Jesus at this point, as I'm not religious at all. It had sounded quite good in my head.

Amber said, 'Well, I think that Jesus actually said something like this –'

Thou shalt not covet thy bestie's boyf

'He's not your boyfriend though, is he!' said Jess.

'And he never will be, thanks to you!' said Amber.

'And you're not my bestie either!' said Jess.

'Also, I'd just like to point out that Jesus actually said "Thou shalt not covet thy neighbour's boyf" . . . and they are not neighbours,' said Poppy. 'They live, like, at least ten minutes' walk away from –'

'Could everyone stop being so pedantic?' I interrupted.

'What does pedantic mean?' asked Jess.

'It means getting overly concerned with small details. It's one of my dad's favourite words. But, anyway, what I am TRYING to say is that if Jesus was here he would like us all to forgive each other and be friends again . . . probably.'

'Well, maybe we could all forgive HER –' Amber pointed at Jess – 'if she promises to keep away from Theo!'

Jess looked at me with wide eyes, as if to say 'What?!?'

So I said, 'Well, I think that sounds totally reasonable, given the circumstances.'

It wasn't reasonable at all, but at this point I was so desperate to get everyone back on good terms that I'd have said anything.

'How is that reasonable?' Jess said. 'Theo and I are just friends and we like playing football sometimes. I don't see why I should have to stay away from him just because you clearly have jealousy issues!'

Amber started going red, puffing her cheeks out and narrowing her eyes.

No, no, no, no, no, nooooo! This wasn't how it was supposed to go. We were meant to be sorting this out like mature young adults.

I think Poppy was equally desperate to sort it out. She looked at me as if to say, 'What the hell do we do now?!'

'I DO NOT HAVE JEALOUSY ISSUES!' yelled Amber.

'And perhaps a few anger-management issues too!'
said Jess.

Amber was deep red by this point. She didn't look unlike
a volcano about to erupt.

(I have drawn her here with steam coming out of her
ears, so you get a good idea of just how furious she
actually looked. I have a feeling that perhaps no one had
ever stood up to her before.)

'Fine. Well, I guess we'll agree to disagree then,' said Jess.

I honestly don't know where Jess was getting all this sass from. Half of me was horrified, while the other half wanted to give her a round of applause for standing up for herself.

'FINE!' shouted Amber. 'AND, JUST TO MAKE IT SUPER CLEAR, WE ARE NOT FRIENDS ANY MORE AND YOU ARE NO LONGER IN THE QUEENS OF SEVEN GREEN!'

OMG!!!!!!!!!!!

'Suits me fine,' said Jess. 'I don't want to be in your stupid, immature little gang anyway.'

OMG!!!!!!!!!!

Then they both stormed off.

Poppy and I were silent, trying to figure out what on earth just happened.

Later on in science I got a pat on the back from Poppy.
She looked at me apologetically and passed me this note.

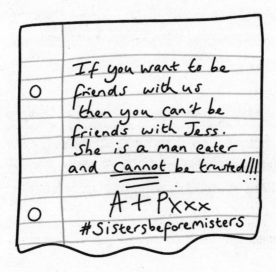

Note how the 'cannot' is underlined three times. Note
the multiple exclamations marks. Poppy and Amber
clearly meant business.

I did a really good job of avoiding everyone for the rest of
the day. At lunchtime I ate my sandwiches perched on the
loo, because I had no idea how to deal with any of this.

When class was over, I grabbed my bag and ran for the
door. I guess Jess had the same idea, as she was already

at the school gates when I got there. I tried to keep my head down, but she grabbed my arm as I walked past.

'Lottie, what's wrong? What have I done? Aren't you speaking to me any more?'

'I just . . . I just . . . I don't know what to do, Jess.'

Then I heard Amber shout from across the road, 'OI, LOTTIE! Are you walking home with us or what?'

I looked up and saw her and Poppy glaring at me.

My heart started to pound. I just wanted the ground to swallow me up.

'Lottie . . . Are we OK?' said Jess.

'I'm sorry,' I whispered, and then I dashed across the road.

Poppy and Amber linked their arms through mine, and we headed off. When I looked back, Jess was standing there, staring at us. She looked so sad that I wanted to cry.

I know what you are thinking of me: What a horrible person! What a coward!

Jess was the first person who reached out to me at school. She is sweet and silly and fun.

I can't even begin to think about telling her that I can't speak to her any more. It's just too awful.

But then I keep remembering **THE PLAN**. I am determined not to mess this up again. I don't want people to make fun of me any more, and being friends with Amber and Poppy will stop that from happening.

And maybe if I keep them onside I can convince Amber and Poppy that Jess isn't interested in Theo and that we should all be friends again? I hope so anyway.

When I got home, I told Mum about the argument, and she looked really sad. She said, 'I just can't understand why you've fallen out with Jess. Good friends are hard to come by, Lottie. Remember that.'

Now I feel even worse.

The hammies tried to counsel me, but it didn't help.

I'm sure there must be some way to fix this. What am I going to do?! I wish you could rewind life and redo the parts that went wrong.

TUESDAY 23 NOVEMBER

Today in science I tried to speak to Amber and Poppy to sort everything out, but they didn't want to listen.

Amber said, 'Look, Lottie. I didn't want to have to tell you this, but Jess is not the friend you think she is. She's been saying mean things about you behind your back for *aaaaaages*.'

'She wouldn't do that . . .' I said.

'It's true, isn't it, Poppy?'

'Yep. She said she thinks you are boring, and that she is only friends with you because she feels sorry for you.'

I felt awful. Does Jess really find me boring? I had to try really hard not to cry.

Amber put her arm round me. 'Look, don't get upset,' she said. 'We don't think you are boring. You still have us!'

'Yes, don't worry, Lottie. We'll always have your back,' said Poppy.

And I guess they were right, as later on I saw Jess eating lunch with Millie and Lily. Then afterwards she was doing keepy-uppies with Theo and his friends, so it seems she's moved on already.

If it had been me who was cast out of the gang, I'm pretty sure I would have been left totally friendless, but everyone seems to love Jess.

I can't help but feel really sad about everything.

At least I have Amber and Poppy. I know I can count on them.

WEDNESDAY 24 NOVEMBER

It's amazing how quickly things can change. A week ago the Queens of Seven Green was a tight foursome. We were getting excited about the school disco and planning our hair and make-up. Now look at us.

Jess was meant to be coming over to my house after school today, but she passed me a note in registration that said: *I'm afraid I don't feel comfortable coming to your house today.*

I had been half hoping that she'd apologize and that would sort everything out, but I guess it really is over. Amber and Poppy were right. Jess truly doesn't care.

I tried to call Molly this evening, but there was no answer. I know I should have called her back sooner, but I doubt she'd be interested in hearing me moan about my boring life anyway. She's probably out surfing or at yet another pool party.

FRIDAY 26 NOVEMBER

Jess was playing footie with the boys again at lunch. If anything, this argument has only pushed her and Theo closer together.

Amber is trying to pretend that she doesn't care at all by repeatedly telling everyone that she doesn't care at all.

I don't think anyone is particularly convinced.

I can feel a storm brewing, and I don't like it.

One good thing is that me, Poppy and Amber made plans to go swimming tomorrow, so I'm excited for that. Hopefully, everything will start to feel normal again soon.

SATURDAY 27 NOVEMBER

Woke up to Mum banging on my bedroom door because I'd slept in. I'd completely forgotten to set my alarm, and Amber and Poppy were waiting for me at the front door.

I jumped out of bed and pulled on my jeans and a sweatshirt, then shoved a towel, my goggles and a swimming costume in my bag.

'BYE, MUM,' I shouted, grabbing a piece of toast with Nutella that she had left out for me before I ran out of the door.

We walked to the King Alfred swimming pool by the beach. (I've been going there since I was tiny!) When we got there, we went into our own individual changing rooms to get ready. Me and Molly always used to share one, but that feels like such a long time ago now. I guess, since we are all starting to grow up, it feels a bit funny stripping off in front of other people. I don't even let my mum see me naked any more, which she seems to find quite funny.

I took off my clothes and underwear, then reached into my bag to get my costume – and this is where it all started to go wrong. In my haste, I'd grabbed one of my REALLY OLD swimsuits. I don't even know what it was still doing in my drawer TBH, as I haven't worn it since I was about seven. Imagine the most embarrassing swimming costume you have ever owned, then times that by ten – no, by 1000. I looked at the costume in utter despair. It was pink and purple, and said 'Cute Lil Cupcake!' on the front, and the absolute worst bit is that it had . . . Oh God, I can hardly bear to tell you this . . . It had an actual tutu attached to it.

Suddenly I felt pretty furious with Mum for buying me such a gender-stereotyped costume in the first place. I mean, if she wants to bring me up to be a feminist, what sort of message does putting me in a frilly pink swimming costume give off?! (I do have a vague memory of lying on the shop floor, screaming at her to get it for me . . . but still. She should have overruled me, right?)

Amber and Poppy started banging on my changing-room door.

'Lottie, come on!' said Amber.

'Do you have your bikini on yet?' said Poppy. 'We're ready to go!'

BIKINI?!? It just gets worse, doesn't it?

'I . . . I have a bit of a problem,' I said.

'What? Did you get your period?!' said Poppy.

'No. Nothing like that. It's just I accidentally packed one of my REALLY OLD swimsuits and, um . . . I don't think it's going to fit. So I won't be able to go swimming after all.'

'Don't be silly!' said Amber. 'Swimsuits are stretchy. It'll be fine. Hurry up, Lottie. We are wasting time. Get it on and let's go.'

I didn't know what else to do, so I did what I was told and put it on. It was tight, but I managed it.

Then I unlocked the door and slowly stepped out. Amber and Poppy looked devastatingly gorgeous in their stylish two-pieces, which made it all **EVEN WORSE**. It took them about fifteen minutes to stop laughing.

When we finally made it out to the pool – with me trying to hide behind walls and other people as much as I could – guess who was there? Theo, Daniel, Tom and Seb! They were standing over by the water slide, and they were staring straight at us.

Amber started sniggering. 'Oh, did we not tell you that the boys usually go swimming on Saturday mornings?'

Errr, no . . . **YOU DID NOT**!

And now they had all seen me looking like this.

The Absolute horror

There was only one thing for it: I jumped into the pool as quickly as possible, in order to hide my swimming costume of shame from public view. And then I stayed there for over an hour, while Amber and Poppy pranced about near the boys, who were practising dives.

I only got out when I was super sure that all the boys had left. By that time I was freezing cold and looked like a prune.

'Lottie, I can't believe you hid in the deep end the entire time,' said Amber as we were leaving. 'It's not because you actually LIKE Daniel, is it?'

I felt my face start to burn.

'OMG, look at her going red! She does! She does!' screeched Poppy.

They proceeded to chant 'Lottie loves Daniel' all the way home, so I'm sure the whole school will know about it on Monday. I'm just really hoping that Daniel didn't see me in my costume!

I think I'll probably need therapy to get over this when I'm older. ☹

Home. Told the family what happened, thinking they might be somewhat sympathetic, but no. They all found it completely hilarious. Traitors.

I have asked Mum to buy me a bikini. I also cut the cupcake swimsuit up into tiny pieces and binned it, to make extra super sure that this **NEVER** happens again.

MONDAY 29 NOVEMBER

So it seems like maybe the boys did see me.

Goodbye, Rice Krispie Head. It was nice knowing you.

TUESDAY 30 NOVEMBER

STOP THE PRESS!

DANIEL FOLLOWED ME ON INSTAGRAM AND
THEN HE SENT ME A DM!!!

Sorry for all the shouting. I'll stop now.

The message said:

> Just for the record, I did think
> you looked cute on Sat. ☺

OMG!

I didn't know what to do, so I just threw my phone across
the room and screamed.

Mum came up to my room to see what was wrong.

I told her I was having a nervous breakdown because a boy had messaged me, which she found hilarious.

(6.30 p.m.)

Spent about two hours composing a reply. Here are a few that were on the shortlist:

* **ARE YOU BLIND OR JUST STUPID?!** (Bit rude?)

* I take it you mean I looked like a deranged ballerina?! (May encourage him to picture me in that hideous costume again. No!)

* Thanks. You looked cute too. (Way too keen.)

In the end I decided on:

Ha. Thanks. Was nice to see you. ☺

(I deliberated for twenty minutes over whether to sign off with a kiss or smiley. I went with a smiley, as a kiss seemed a bit too romantic and I'm not sure I want to give him that impression just yet.)

He's replied **ALREADY**!

This was what he sent:

A smiley **AND** a kiss! What could it possibly mean?!?

WEDNESDAY 1 DECEMBER

I can't believe it's December. The start of the festive
season. A time for joy and cheer!

Except that the whole of Year Seven is still taking much
delight in calling me Cute Lil Cupcake, and Mum has
bought me one of those cheap own-brand Advent
calendars with chocolates that taste like soap.
I specifically asked for a Celebrations one too! ☹

Toby doesn't seem to care though. He got up at 5 a.m.
and wolfed the lot of his in one go. The boy clearly
doesn't have any taste buds.

Mum didn't get as cross as I'd expected her to. She just said, 'Well, he's the one who will regret it when there is nothing to open tomorrow.'

Honestly, that boy gets away with murder.

Oh also, guess what? Daniel smiled at me in the corridor today! I felt a bit light-headed. Do you think that means I actually like him?!

I can't tell Amber and Poppy though, as I know they'll just laugh. Sometimes I really wish Jess and I were still talking.

THURSDAY 2 DECEMBER

Mum was right. Toby is now in a state of deep regret.

Seeing as I don't like the chocolate in my calendar, I
have decided to sell him a piece for 25p a day. I can
then spend the 25p on a Cadbury's Freddo from the
newsagent's on the way to school. Toby is too stupid to
see through my clever ruse. Not just a pretty face, huh?

Anyway, back to the more exciting news, because
the word on the street is that Jess and Theo are now
boyfriend and girlfriend!

Leah told Mia, who told Lily, who told Millie, who told
Chloe, who told Zoe, who told Miley, who told Kylie,
who told Amber, who told me (I think I got that right)
that she saw them snogging each other's faces off by
the science block.

I mean, it doesn't sound much like Jess, but you can
hardly refute the word of a ninth-hand eyewitness,
can you?

Amber spent all lunchtime crying in the loos. She says
she can't believe that Jess is 'flaunting their happiness'
in her face and that Jess should have much more respect
for her feelings.

I have to admit I am pretty shocked too. Jess did know
how much Amber liked Theo, so it seems pretty unkind
of her to get together with him so quickly.

Amber says she has a plan. Poppy and I are meeting her
in the form room at 8.30 a.m. tomorrow.

I'm scared to go, yet also too scared not to go.

GULP.

FRIDAY 3 DECEMBER

When I got to the form room this morning, Amber
and Poppy were already there. They had written
JESS LOVES THEO in massive letters on the
whiteboard and couldn't stop giggling.

'Great, you're here. You have to draw them kissing by the
science block underneath,' said Amber.

'Yeh, come on. You're the artist!' said Poppy.

My stomach flipped. 'I'm not sure . . .' I said. It didn't feel
right at all.

'It's just a joke,' said Amber. 'Everyone will think it's
hilarious. We'll rub it off before Mr Peters arrives,
I swear.'

I wanted to run right out of the room, but I couldn't say
no, could I? If I didn't have Amber and Poppy, then I'd
have no friends at all!

'OK . . .' I said, picking up the marker pen. 'But we've got to rub it right off.'

This is what I drew. I mean, I have to admit I did a pretty good job, even if I do say so myself!

'Now quick! Sit down before everyone comes in,' said Poppy.

'But we have to rub it off,' I said.

'Yes, we will before Mr Peters arrives,' Amber said.
'Sit down.'

All the kids started filing in. As soon as they saw the picture, they started laughing and wolf-whistling and making kissing sounds.

It did feel quite good to see everyone laughing at my picture. But that was before Jess arrived. When she walked into the room, everyone burst out laughing. She looked so confused.

'Look behind you, Jess!' someone called out.

She turned round and looked at the board, then straight away put her head down. She looked like she was going to cry. She hurried to her seat and started chewing the sleeves of her blazer – just like I do when I feel nervous.

I knew she'd recognize the drawing as mine. I felt like the worst person in the world.

I ran to the front of the class and grabbed the whiteboard eraser, then started wiping the board clean – but I'd barely begun before Mr Peters arrived. He looked at the board, then over at Jess, who was desperately fighting back the tears, and then he looked at me, holding the eraser.

'Lottie, are you responsible for this?' he asked in a super-serious voice.

The room was dead silent. I looked over at Amber and Poppy. They both had their heads down.

'I . . . I . . .' I looked down at my hands, which were covered in marker pen.

I'd been caught red-handed. Literally.

There was nothing else I could do, so I just nodded my head. I was too ashamed of myself to speak.

Mr Peters sighed and looked really disappointed.

'Stay behind after registration,' he said. 'Now go and sit down. Jess, I'd like you to stay behind too.'

'Yes, sir,' she whispered.

After registration, when the rest of the class got up to leave, I secretly hoped Amber and Poppy would stay behind too – but Amber just whispered in my ear on her way past, 'Remember no one likes a snitch.'

'What is this all about?' Mr Peters asked when everyone had gone.

'It was just supposed to be a joke, sir,' I said.

'Do you think Jess found it funny?'

'No, sir.'

'Well, would you like to apologize to her?'

'I'm so sorry, Jess,' I said. 'I don't know why I did it. I wish I could take it back.'

I really meant it.

'OK,' Jess whispered without looking at me.

'This isn't like you, Lottie,' said Mr Peters. 'Was it your idea? If anyone else was involved, I'd suggest it would be a good idea to come clean now.'

'No, sir . . .' I said. 'It was just me.'

'Well then, I'm afraid I'm going to have to put you on lunchtime detention every day next week. If anything like this happens again, I shall be calling your parents. The school has a very strict anti-bullying policy. Is that clear?'

'Yes, sir.'

'Right, well, off to class, both of you.'

After we left the room, I tried to speak to Jess, but she just shrugged me off and ran down the corridor.

I felt horrible for the rest of the day.

I'm not a bully. Am I?

Poppy and Amber didn't seem to get it. Poppy just said, 'Lighten up, Lottie. You only got detention. We didn't kill anyone!'

'It wasn't even my idea though,' I replied.

Amber gave a huge sigh and shook her head. 'I didn't realize you were such a baby, Lottie. Grow up!'

It felt like she had slapped me in the face. Poppy just shook her head too, then they walked off together, leaving me alone.

I thought they were meant to be my friends. But if they were proper friends they wouldn't leave me to take the blame, would they? It's like they've just thrown me under the bus.

I so badly want to speak to Molly, as she always gives the best advice, but things feel different between us lately. It's like we've grown apart, and I've lost my BFF too.

6.23 p.m.

Mum and Dad know.

Apparently my detentions have shown up on that stupid school app that they basically use to stalk us.

The worst thing is that they didn't even seem angry. They just said that they were 'really disappointed', which, in a way, felt a lot worse. They said I've let everyone down – including myself.

I can't even argue with them, as I know they are right.

As punishment, I have been grounded and (this is the real killer) **THEY HAVE CHANGED THE WI-FI PASSWORD**.

What on earth am I meant to do with myself now?! I mean, those YouTube make-up tutorials won't watch themselves, will they?

Woe is me.

SATURDAY 4 DECEMBER

No friends. No phone. No internet. **NO TIKTOK!**

I can't even enjoy feeling sorry for myself by looking at how happy other people are on Instagram. This is a form of torture.

I have heard nothing from Poppy or Amber. I thought maybe they would have called by to see how I was. Maybe they've sent a WhatsApp? Only I can't check, can I?

It's strange. Now I have all the time in the world to write in my diary but literally nothing interesting to report.

SUNDAY 5 DECEMBER

 9.07 a.m.

Decided to eat a banana.

 9.14 a.m.

Finished banana. Not as enjoyable as I had hoped. Bit brown in places.

 11.14 a.m.

Bit a fingernail, then it ripped off really low down. It properly hurts now!

12.13 p.m.

There are 237 polka dots on my bedroom curtains.

1.24 p.m.

Squirrels are pretty cool, aren't they? Must be really nice to be able to climb trees so fast.

2.29 p.m.

Just spent forty-five minutes daydreaming about sloths. They are just the absolute cutest! If I had to be an animal, I'd defo be a sloth.

2.35 p.m

Or possibly an orca . . . or a red panda . . . or a tiger.
GRRRRRRRRR!

3.55 p.m.

If I was a biscuit, I'd be a custard cream.

4.02 p.m.

Changed my mind. I'd be a chocolate finger.

4.16 p.m.

What was I thinking? I'd obviously be a Jammie Dodger!

5.55 p.m.

Where do hair bobbles go? They seem to just disappear into thin air! I had a new ten-pack just last week and now I only have one left. Maybe Toby is eating them?!?

6.15 p.m.

Had lasagne for dinner. A strange meal, if you stop and think about it. It's basically spaghetti-flavoured cake, isn't it?

7.49 p.m.

OMG, what did people even do before Wi-Fi was invented?!? Life must have been soooo boring!

8.15 p.m.

Started thinking about how massive space is and got really freaked out. I think I'd better go to bed now. Goodnight!

MONDAY 6 DECEMBER

Today was a long and uneventful day at school.

Caught Daniel's eye in science over a Bunsen burner, and
he gave me a sort of pitying half smile. I guess he's on
#TEAMJESS then. Or maybe he never even liked me in
the first place . . .

Had detention at lunch. Mr Peters made me write 200
lines saying, *I must not bring my friendship dramas into the
classroom*, which I felt was a little patronizing.

Apart from in class, I barely saw Amber or Poppy at all.
I thought maybe they'd be waiting for me at the end of
the day, but by the time I got out of my last period they
were nowhere to be seen, so I had to walk home alone.

WEDNESDAY 8 DECEMBER

Mr Peters gave me a maths problem to solve in detention today.

Bernard has 130 balloons.

$\frac{2}{3}$ of the blue balloons burst.

$\frac{2}{5}$ of the red balloons burst.

There are now 36 more red balloons than blue ones.

How many balloons are left in total?

It made my head want to explode!

WHAT I WANT TO KNOW IS:

* Why did Bernard have such an excessive number of balloons in the first place?

* How did Bernard manage to burst so many of them? He sounds very careless.

* Is Bernard not aware of the damaging impact balloons have on the environment?

* And most importantly . . .

Mr Peters said that you can't answer maths problems with more questions, but I could see him trying not to laugh so I think he liked my answers a little bit.

THURSDAY 9 DECEMBER

A haiku by Lottie Brooks, age 12.

The days seem endless.

My KitKat Chunky tastes bitter.

I still have no boobs.

THOUGHT OF THE DAY:
I am so bored and isolated that
I am writing poetry! What have
I been reduced to?!

FRIDAY 10 DECEMBER

I've hardly spoken to anyone in school all week, apart from Mr Peters – but teachers don't count as real people, do they?

Every day after school I've looked for Amber and Poppy, and every day they've been nowhere to be seen. They know I've been stuck in detention. It's like they don't even care . . . which seems really unfair, as it's partly their fault I'm there in the first place.

To top it all off, the Freddo ruse is sadly over. Mum caught Toby emptying his piggy bank and he blabbed. Mum says I owe Toby £2 and this will come out of my pocket money.

Sad times.

SATURDAY 11 DECEMBER

Turns out being grounded only includes not being allowed to go and see my friends. Family days out are still compulsory.

Today we went to visit Father Christmas, because my parents have apparently forgotten that, now I am twelve years old, I no longer believe that Santa's Workshop is based in the Greenfingers Garden Centre on the A24.

I did the big thing though and went along with it for Toby's benefit. I even wrote a letter to put in the Special North Pole Postbox because, although I am **VERY** sceptical indeed, I don't want to jinx anything, do I?

Dear F.C

I have been really good this year (mostly) please could you make/buy/whatever it is you do, me:

1. A frappuccino machine

2. The latest iphone with un-limited data plan

3. My own credit card

4. A personality transplant for my little brother

5. Some sort of sign of puberty anything will do, except body odour.

6. Lifetime supply of kitkat chunkys

7. friends who like me again

Cheers mate, love Lottie X

SUNDAY 12 DECEMBER

After dinner Mum handed my phone back to me.

I switched it on, the screen lit up, and I looked at all the apps for notifications to see what I'd missed.

First, I checked Instagram. I saw a selfie of Amber and Poppy in Starbucks, and the caption said: **AWESOME TIME SHOPPING WITH MY BESTIE! #BFFS4EVA**. It was like a punch in the gut.

I double-checked WhatsApp. No messages.

I've been sitting at home alone all weekend and they've been hanging out together, having fun, like nothing has happened. They didn't come over to see me or even send me a text to see if I was OK . . .

I kept scrolling. I saw a picture of Jess and Florence at the park, grinning at the camera. I saw a photo of Molly and Isla lying on lilos in the pool. I saw Theo and Daniel wrapped up in scarves, eating chips at a football match. I saw Liv showing off an incredible hot-pink-and-neon-orange ombré manicure. I saw photos of all the celebs I follow looking super glamorous, and the screen started to blur and I realized I was crying.

The notifications kept going off, so I put my phone out of reach and got into bed.

I wish I had never even got it back. It's just made me feel really lonely.

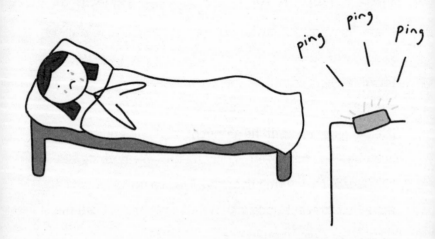

TUESDAY 14 DECEMBER

The last couple of days have been really tough.

Amber and Poppy have been totally blanking me, and I just don't get it. Every time I see them, they spin round and walk off, laughing. I have no idea what I'm supposed to have done. It's like they got what they wanted, and now they have no interest in me any more.

So I've gone full circle and am back to eating my sandwiches alone in the loos again.

I saw Theo on the way home from school. I was trying to keep my head down, but he had clearly been looking out for me.

'Hey, Cucumber Girl!' he shouted.

'Oh, hey,' I said, trying to sound dead casual. 'It's actually Cute Lil Cupcake now, but you can still call me Cucumber Girl, if you like . . .'

'You'll always be a cucumber to me,' he said, laughing.

I smiled and started to walk away.

'It's not true, you know,' he called after me.

'What's not true?'

'About me and Jess . . . you know . . . That's just some dumb rumour Amber started.'

'But Amber said . . .'

'Amber lied. Me and Jess are just friends.'

'Really?'

'Yes, really. I don't have time for girlfriends right now anyway. I've got to spend all my spare time training if I'm going to make it in the prem.'

'The prem?'

'Yeh, I'm going to be a premiership footballer.'

'Oh, yeh. Of course . . . totally . . .'

'You don't sound convinced, Cucumber Girl. Watch and see.' He winked at me.

And then he dashed off, doing keepy-uppies as he went. He's getting pretty good, but still nowhere near as good as Jess.

'Oh, Theo,' I called after him. 'I just wanted to say . . . I'm sorry. That's all.'

'We're cool, Cucumber Girl. Maybe you should tell Jess though.'

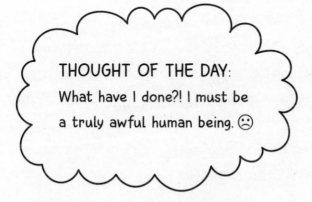

THOUGHT OF THE DAY:
What have I done?! I must be
a truly awful human being. ☹

WEDNESDAY 15 DECEMBER

I decided to send Liv an emergency text.

> **ME:** SOS! I seem to have messed everything up and I have no friends left. I need to employ you as my PR manager. Please help!! xx

> **LIV:** I'll be over straight after school! xx

When she arrived, I made us both a cup of coffee and pretended to like it, just like last time. I explained everything that had happened at the disco and with the whiteboard drawing, while Liv listened carefully, nodding her head.

'The thing is, Lottie, I think you've just been trying too hard,' she said when I'd finished.

'I just wanted to be one of the popular gang,' I said sadly.

'Why do you think Amber and Poppy are popular though?'

'What do you mean?'

'I mean, they don't sound very nice. It sounds like they're only popular because people are scared of them. Do you really want friends like that? Is that how you want people to see you?'

'No! I'd never want that.'

'And why do you think Jess is popular?'

'Because she's cool and she's funny and she's kind . . . Oh . . .'

And suddenly everything started to make sense. I've been so obsessed with trying to be popular that I've forgotten about making friends with people who I actually like and who actually like me.

'Lottie, why do you grimace every time you take a sip of coffee?' Liv said, interrupting my thoughts.

'Because I . . . well . . . I don't actually like it very much . . .'

'Why are you drinking it then?!'

'Because I guess I wanted you to think –'

'This is exactly what I'm trying to say! Be yourself and stop trying so hard. It's so much easier.'

THURSDAY 16 DECEMBER

AKA the worst day ever.

I woke up feeling vaguely positive about stuff today. Or
at least OK. I thought that maybe I'd be able to try and
sort a few things out, but the day started badly and got
progressively worse.

Firstly, a bird pooed on my head on the way to school.
I tried to wash it off in the loos, but it was really hard
without any shampoo, so I just had bird poo streaked
hair all day.

Then I made a loaf of bread in home economics, and I
have no idea how but it ended up looking like a pair of
big boobs. Even loaves of bread are taunting my flat-
chestedness now!

why does this sort of thing always happen to me?!?

Next, I discovered that Dad had mixed my sandwiches up with Toby's so, instead of my usual cheese, I had Marmite and jam. (I am not joking. That is what he actually eats!)

Then we did yoga during PE and I farted (loudly) while doing the downward dog. Probably due, in part, to the Marmite and jam sandwiches I'd had to force down. (I was starving, OK!)

Amber was on a mat right behind me, and she went,
'OH, LOTTIE! THAT IS SO DISGUSTING! WHAT HAVE
YOU BEEN EATING?!'

Then the whole class burst out laughing and started
wafting the air around them. My cheeks were burning so
much I could hardly deny it was me. I caught Jess's eye
and saw she was laughing along with everyone else, and
it really hurt.

Amber, Poppy, Jess – none of them want to be seen dead
with me any more.

And Molly has an exciting new life that I can't begin to compete with.

PS We ate some of my boob bread with dinner and everyone thought it was delicious, so I guess that's one good thing to come out of today. Toby actually said, 'This is the best breasty bread I've ever had!'

FRIDAY 17 DECEMBER

Today was the last day of school, and I was so glad to see the back of it. I've ended the term totally friendless and I have only myself to blame.

I got so obsessed with being popular that I couldn't see the wood for the trees. Or the friends for the fake friends, or however you want to look at it.

Poppy and Amber left arm in arm. Jess and Theo went off for a kick-about. Daniel said a quick, 'Have a good Christmas, Lottie.' Then I walked home alone, just like I do every day.

To make matters worse, it then began to absolutely tip it down, and my coat had no hood and I had no umbrella. I started to run home as quickly as I could, but my bag was so super heavy with all my textbooks in it that it broke, and the buckle on the strap pinged off and hit me in the face! It hurt a lot more than you might imagine.

I opened the door looking like a drowned rat, with a bleeding face, and when Mum saw me she said, 'Lottie! Oh, darling, what's wrong?' and then I started crying and couldn't seem to stop.

Mum said she'd make me a nice hot chocolate to warm me up, and she got me a towel and some clean PJs. It turned out we were out of hot chocolate **AND** milk **AND** marshmallows though, so instead I had to have a hot lemon squash (which was actually relatively pleasant).

When I was warm and dry again, with a towel round my head and snuggled under a cosy blanket, Mum asked me why I was so upset.

'No one likes me. Everyone is laughing at me,' I said. 'I have no friends, stupid bird legs, boring hair, no personality and . . . and . . . I'm just a big old farty pants!'

'Stop it, Lottie, please. Do you know how sad it makes me to hear you say those things about yourself? Do you know how hard it is for me to hear that you cannot see how amazing you are? Do you know how proud I am of you? You are smart and kind, and you are so funny! You make us laugh every day, Lottie. And you are so beautiful – you are beautiful because you are you, because of your cute little nose and freckles, which I adore, and your eyes that are so blue I could swim in them. I love you just the way you are, and anyone who can't see how amazing you are isn't worth your tears. I promise.'

Then she got me a KitKat Chunky to help cheer me up, and I told her about Jess and all the mistakes that I had made, and Mum promised to help me fix it.

Afterwards I felt so much better about everything. Ev~ if I did look like a sobbing, chocolatey mess.

THOUGHT OF THE DAY:

I honestly don't know what I'd do without KitKat Chunkys. They've seen me through some properly dark times. If I had to rank them against my family members, it'd probably go:

1. Mum

2. KitKat Chunkys

3. Dad

4. Professor Barnaby Squeakington and Fuzzball the 3rd

5. Toby.

SATURDAY 18 DECEMBER

At breakfast, Mum announced, 'I've got a great surprise for you all. We are going ice-skating at Brighton Pavilion!'

It wasn't a *great* surprise, as none of us actually like ice-skating that much. Does anyone actually like ice-skating?! I mean, it's really difficult, you just end up falling on your arse all the time, it's cold, the boots always hurt your feet, and there is that worry that you are going to get your fingers sliced off by somebody else's blades. (Not sure if that's ever actually happened? But still, it seems like a big risk to take if you value your fingers – which I do.)

Mum is probably happy about it because she's pregnant, so she won't actually have to do it. Instead, she'll be taking photos and sipping a nice hot drink in the comfort of the bar, then posting the photos on Facebook to show what a happy, wholesome family we really are!

I AM SO HAPPY!!!!!

Today was the **BEST DAY EVER**. Well, maybe not quite
as good as 6 June 2018 when I got the closest guess for
the number of bubblegums in a massive jar (1,518) and
won the lot! That was epic.

But still, it was pretty close.

We arrived at the pavilion just after sunset. It was all
lit up with pink and purple lights, and looked so pretty

and Christmassy. I was still trying to be in a bad mood though, so I put on my skates and grumpily made my way over to the ice – and guess who was there? Jess!

My mum, the sneaky trickster, had called Jess's mum and organized to meet us there.

At first, I was all like, 'OH NO! Jess is over there. I must quickly find a cave to hide in,' but by then Roxanne had already seen me and was waving me over.

There wasn't much else I could do but slowly (and very badly) start skating over to them. Next thing I knew, I was knocked flying by a teenage boy who was skating backwards at about 100 miles per hour. I landed on my bum, right by Roxanne's feet. Mega embarrassing!

'Lottie,' she said. 'We've missed you so much! Are you OK?' She pulled me up and gave me a hug.

'I'm fine.' I smiled, trying to ignore my bruised butt.

'OTTIE, UDDLES!' said Florence, clinging to my leg. I gave her a squeeze and it felt so good. Jess's family have always been so welcoming to me. I didn't realize how much I'd missed them all.

'Hi, Jess,' I said nervously, not quite managing to look her in the eyes.

'Hi, Lottie,' she said, scuffing her boots on the ice.

'I'll leave you guys to catch up. I've got to find a penguin to help Florence skate,' said Roxanne.

Jess looked kind of horrified. I guess she hadn't been involved in our mothers' blatant scheming either.

It felt really awkward. I had so much I wanted to say, but no idea how to get the words out.

'I can't believe they set us up like this . . .' I finally started.

'I know! I thought Mum was acting shifty . . .' said Jess.

'I mean, who do they think they are, interfering in our lives like this?'

'I know! How old do they think we are? Five?!'

We laughed, and then it went silent again for a minute before we both opened our mouths and blurted at exactly the same time, 'I'm so sorry!'

'I'm the one who should be sorry,' I said. 'I never should have chosen to be friends with Amber and Poppy over you. And I feel awful for drawing that stupid picture. It's just that they said you were only friends with me because you felt sorry for me . . .'

'I'd never say that! I loved being friends with you, Lottie!'

'I know that now. I was so silly to believe them . . . I just wanted to be part of their gang so badly that I couldn't see how mean they were. I was scared of being Matey McLobster Legs again.'

'Lottie, what on earth are you talking about? Who is Matey McLobster Legs?!'

'It's a long story!'

'OK. Well, I'd love to hear it some time,' said Jess, smiling. 'And I'm sorry too, for not talking to you last week when I knew you were having a hard time, and for laughing at you when you . . . you know . . . in yoga.'

'When I did that massive fart, you mean?' I said, and then we both got the giggles.

'I've really missed you, Lottie.'

'I've really missed you too, Jess.'

And, just like that, we were friends again. We skated arm in arm until our session was up. Plus, with a little practice, it turned out both of us were much better at ice-skating than we had remembered. We looked a bit like Torvill and Dean out there . . .

THOUGHT OF THE DAY:
Maybe I could make it as a professional
ice-skater?!* Then I could give up school
and tour the world in one of those
massive buses celebrities have, with beds
and fridges and stuff.

*Googled it and apparently I should have been enrolled in an
ice-skating academy from the age of four. So thanks, Mum and
Dad, for not spotting my potential earlier on. I wish I had pushy
parents . . . Mine just seem content to let me fly by the seat of
my pants.

MONDAY 20 DECEMBER

My granny and grandad are coming to stay over
Christmas. This is really good for me, as they always buy
me and Toby great presents. It is less good for Mum as,
according to her, Granny 'criticizes literally everything
I do'. Grandad is fine though, as he doesn't really make
any noises other than to snore or grunt.

Mum is already stressing massively about the turkey,
which is ridiculous. I don't understand why adults get
so stressed about turkey at Christmas. No one wants to
eat turkey any other day of the year, so why do they go
crazy for it at Christmas?! It's not even very nice, and
it costs about ten times as much as a chicken does. For
some strange reason, you also have to order it weeks
in advance, but whenever you go into any supermarket
there are always huge numbers of them just sitting there
on the shelves. Go figure. Whenever I query any of these
points, Mum doesn't seem to be to able give any logical

answers. She just says, 'Oh, you'll get it when you are older, Lottie,' and shakes her head. Bizarre.

I won't get it when I'm older. I'll just serve up frozen pizza, as I much prefer it to Christmas dinner anyway. Quicker, easier, cheaper and everyone's satisfied!

Maybe I'll get those posh Pizza Express ones and give everyone a whole pizza each, just in case people think I'm being stingy. Oh . . . and a whole packet of dough balls each too. It is Christmas after all.

TUESDAY 21 DECEMBER

Stop the press. Something noteworthy has actually happened!

It was just another normal morning and I'd had a nice, normal shower. It was as I was putting my underwear on afterwards that I first noticed it. There it was – a pubic hair! ☺

In the interests of full disclosure it was very fine and almost invisible to the naked eye, but still . . .

It is official. Puberty has finally begun.

I mean, I'd rather have got boobs instead, but I guess beggars can't be choosers.

After getting dressed, I went downstairs and I must have

been wandering about the house looking a bit spaced out, as Mum said, 'What's up, Lottie? You look a bit different today.'

'Different how?' I said.

Could she actually tell?

'I'm not sure. Maybe you are just looking a bit more grown-up all of a sudden.'

I wasn't sure whether I should tell her, but then I just blurted it out. 'Mum, I think I've got a new hair . . .'

'What do you mean, you've got a new hair, darling?' She looked confused.

'You know, a new hair . . . down there.'

As soon as I'd said it, I immediately regretted it.

'Oooooooh, my baby! I can't believe it!' she squealed, giving me a big hug. 'What shall we do to celebrate?'

'Um . . . I dunno if we need to celebrate it, Mum. It's just one singular pubic hair.'

I knew **EXACTLY** what she was about to start banging on about.

'It is a big deal though, Lottie! It's the start of your journey into woman–'

'MUM!' I said.

'OK, sorry, love. No more about journeys into womanhood, I promise.'

And we both laughed.

In the end, we agreed on getting takeaway Starbucks. I got a strawberry Frappuccino and a cake-pop, and Mum got a latte and a chocolate brownie.

We were at the kitchen table, eating our cakes and drinking our drinks, when Dad and Toby came home.

I shot Mum a warning look, before she opened her mouth to tell him the finer details.

'Lottie,' she said. 'We are just celebrating our wonderful Lottie.'

So that's the story of the day I officially started puberty and we ended up having a pubic-hair tea party.

THOUGHT OF THE DAY:
Can't help wondering if this 'new development' had something to do with Santa . . . Did he actually read my letter?! Maybe he is real after all!

FRIDAY 24 DECEMBER
(AKA CHRISTMAS EVE!)

Granny and Grandad have arrived. Things didn't get off
to the best of starts.

Mum doesn't like people commenting on how **MASSIVE** she is, for some reason.

I, however, was thrilled to see Granny and Grandad, as they said I could open their present early, and guess what it was? AirPods! Wow! I love them so much! I also love Granny and Grandad so much for buying them for me. My parents are way too stingy to get me any.

4.12 p.m.

Me and Jess have just got back from doing our Christmas shopping. I always do all mine on Christmas Eve and it's fine.

However, I did run into one problem. When I counted out the money in my piggy bank, there was only £7.27 left. I had seemingly spent it all on flavoured lip gloss and KitKat Chunkys without noticing. Luckily, I managed to 'borrow' thirty quid off Dad and this is what I bought:

* **TOBY**: An alien foetus in slime and a rainbow-poo squishy.

* **DAD**: Aftershave called 'REAL SPICY MAN' from the pound shop.

* **GRANNY**: Corn plasters for her feet and a 'Grow Your Own Jesus' kit.

* **GRANDAD**: A book called 101 *Things to Do Before You Die*.

* **THE HAMMIES**: Ariana Grande body mist. (OK, that may be for me, but they'd be happy with a loo roll so it seemed like a waste to get them anything.)

* **MUM**: A mug with a picture of a massive dinosaur on it that says 'Pregasaurus'. Hilarious. I think she'll love it.

Then Jess and I realized that we hadn't got each other anything. So we had the idea of getting a necklace that we could keep forever. We looked in the jewellery store and found one that was just perfect! It is a little heart that splits into two, and each half is on its own chain, and I think it describes us both pretty well. Don't you?

Had a lovely Christmas Eve. We all watched *Elf* with the fire on and ate lots of sausage rolls and mince pies. I honestly don't know why adults get so stressed about Christmas. I always find it dead relaxing.

Dear God, Toby is being a nightmare. He won't stay in bed as he is too excited. I bet you anything he will also wake up at 5 a.m., screaming the house down with chants of 'HE'S BEEN! HE'S BEEN! HE'S BEEN!' He is **SO** immature.

Couldn't sleep, so went down for a glass of water and caught Dad red-handed, snaffling all the mince pies and gin we'd left out for FC! Bloomin' cheek of him.

(Note that he left the carrot, which I will bring up if he starts nagging me about eating my veg tomorrow.)

SATURDAY 25 DECEMBER

(AKA CHRISTMAS DAY!)

I know it may be a tad early, but ...

(10.37 a.m.)

OMG! So, I may have got a little over excited, but I got SO many great Christmas presents. OMG! Father Christmas, you are the best! I mean, Mum and Dad. Or whoever it is that gets the presents under the tree. I don't really care who gets them, TBH, as long as they are there.

THIS IS WHAT I GOT:

* a Polaroid camera

* three packs of film

* Greta Thunberg's book – *No One Is Too Small to Make a Difference*

* an actual proper make-up set!

* lots of nice smellies

* unicorn slippers

OMG! I love Christmas.

Granny says I should shop saying OMG so much, as it's blasphemous and not particularly suitable to be saying on Christmas Day. I don't understand how it's blasphemous if I'm saying it in a good way. I mean it's like, 'Oh, God, thank you so much for giving life to Jesus so we could all get such excellent presents,' and that's a good thing, right?

Granny says that getting presents is not the true meaning of Christmas, but I think Christmas means different things to different people, and anyway she seemed pretty pleased with her extra-cosy foot warmer from Mum and Dad.

(**11.12 a.m.**)

Not everyone is as pleased as I am with their presents.

Dad got Mum a book called *The Mindful Guide to a Positive Pregnancy*, which was full of calming exercises and mindfulness techniques that mums-to-be can use to avoid stress. It seemed like a pretty thoughtful gift to me, but Mum looked a bit like she wanted to hit Dad over the head with it. Further evidence that she does need that book!

He also got her a new whisk, but she didn't seem to like
that much either.

Poor Mum's not having the best day. She looked a little
sad at lunch, because the turkey was not quite as juicy
as she'd hoped. Luckily, Granny was there to point this
out to everyone so Mum can do a better job of cooking it
next year.

I knew we should have had pizza!

After dinner, Mum said she was going for a lie-down in a dark room and told us not to disturb her unless it was urgent. And no, asking her if we had any more Doritos did not fit into the urgent category (as I quickly found out).

6.27 p.m.

I GOT A TEXT FROM DANIEL!

> Happy Christmas, Lottie. Hear you
> sorted stuff out with Jess. That's
> great news! See you in the New Year.
> D xx

OH MY LIFE! Kisses and everything. ARGHHHHHHH.

Right, off to phone Jess, so we can dissect every word.

(8.11 p.m.)

Got dragged off the phone by Mum, because apparently 'it's rude to spend so long talking to a friend on Christmas Day'.

We'd only been chatting for one and a half hours!

I said, 'Well, Mum, it's not every day you get a text from a boy you might like, is it?'

She smiled and looked off into the distance. I guess she's probably feeling a bit jealous because the only texts she ever gets are from Dad saying stuff like, *We need bog roll*.

SUNDAY 26 DECEMBER
(AKA BOXING DAY)

Granny is giving the house 'a proper clean', because apparently it's 'really quite dusty'.

Dad told Mum, 'She's just trying to be helpful!' and then Mum did actually throw the mindfulness book at him.

Me, Toby and Grandpa are hiding in the living room, watching Christmas telly and enjoying our Boxing Day diet, which consists of:

cheesy balls

twiglets

After eights

mince pies

chocolate orange

Quality street

pringles

YUM!

I love Boxing Day.

It's my favourite.

CHRIMBO LIMBO
(AKA I HAVE NO IDEA WHAT DAY OR DATE IT IS, AND NOR DO I CARE)

Granny and Grandad have left. Mum is visibly more relaxed.

No one has properly seen Toby for days. We think he is now living in the airing cupboard, surviving on a diet of Fruit Shoots, dry-roasted peanuts and Ferrero Rocher, but it's hard to say for sure.

Dad keeps trying to convince us to go out for a 'nice Christmas walk', because he is insane. I think he just wants to go to the pub but won't admit it.

Luckily, Mum is so massive now that she doesn't really want to do very much. So she and I just fill the hours cuddling up, watching movies and stuffing our faces. We have absolutely zero idea what day of the week it is, and nor do we care. Bliss!

#LIVINGOURBESTLIVES

FRIDAY 31 DECEMBER

For the first time ever, Mum and Dad said that I could stay up until midnight to see in the New Year, but it was kind of pointless because they had half a glass of prosecco each and then fell asleep on the sofa by 11 p.m. Pathetic!

I ended up going to my room to celebrate with my hammies instead. And do you know what? It felt kind of perfect.

SATURDAY 1 JANUARY

Today is the start of a new year – a blank canvas and all that.

Mum says she doesn't believe in resolutions because 'there is no better you than you, and putting pressure on yourself to change isn't healthy'. Boy, do I know that!

So I'm not going to change anything about myself.

Instead, I'm going to do more to change the world for the better, à la Greta Thunberg! I finished reading her book last night and it was epic.

THEREFORE, MY NEW YEAR'S RESOLUTIONS ARE AS FOLLOWS:

1. Try being vegan for a ~~month week~~ day.

2. Cut down on the amount of single-use plastic we use as a household.

3. Go litter-picking regularly.

4. Go to a climate change protest with a really cool sign.

5. Generally get really woke about planet stuff.

In short, I'm going to become . . . .

ECO WARRIOR GIRL!

Recycle losers!

Dad said they were excellent resolutions and that he was really proud of me. Mum seemed happy too, until I started going through the kitchen cupboards and highlighting all the problems with the things she's been buying.

SUNDAY 2 JANUARY

Dad woke me up way too early. All toasty-cosy in my bed,
I was!

He said there was a litter-pick going on at the beach to
help clear up after all the New Year's Eve revellers, and
they were meeting at the pier at 9 a.m.

'If you jump in the shower really quickly, Lottie, we'll be
able to make it!'

I said, 'WHOA THERE! Look, Dad, I'm obviously very
concerned about pollution, but I'm also very concerned
about how cold it will be out there. I mean, I am
committed to becoming an eco-warrior, but you have to
ease yourself into these things, don't you? I can hardly
be expected to save the entire planet in one day, can I?'

Plus, Greta is doing a really great job right now, and I
wouldn't want to tread on her toes.

It's back to school tomorrow, and I'm not going to lie: I have been feeling quite terrified about seeing Amber and Poppy again.

Jess came round this afternoon and gave me a great pep talk.

She said, 'Look, Lottie, you are brilliant, you are clever, you are funny and, above all else, you are a Cute Lil Cupcake. Work it!'

I cannot believe that I ever doubted this girl.

We made a plan to meet before school and go in together, necklaces on and heads held high.

PS Also a teeny-tiny bit excited about seeing Daniel.

MONDAY 3 JANUARY

'Are you ready?' Jess said when I met her at school.

'I think so,' I said, smiling back at her.

We linked arms, then walked into school and pushed open the door of our form room.

we're weirdos and we own it :)

I tried not to focus on Amber and Poppy, but it's very hard not to as they always have a crowd around them. And they were standing right in the path to my desk.

'Excuse me,' I said.

Amber spun round and gave me her full attention.

'Excuse you?! Why? You aren't going to fart on me again, are you, Lottie?' she announced loudly to the class with a smirk.

There were a few little giggles, then everyone went silent, waiting to hear what I'd say.

I felt the panic start to rise in my chest, but I knew that was exactly what Amber wanted. This was my one shot to tell her I wasn't going to bow down to her any more.

So this is what I said:

(I'll have to thank Toby for that line later. I guess little brothers do have their uses after all.)

The entire class cracked up laughing, and for once Amber was completely lost for words. She looked pretty annoyed.

I just smiled sweetly and took my seat.

And do you know what? The rest of the day was just fine.

Did Amber and Poppy try and make me feel small? No, they did not.

Did anyone else laugh at me? No, they did not.

Did anyone else comment on the hideously embarrassing yoga fart? Not to my face!

Did anything bad happen at all? **NOPE!**

In fact, some kids I hardly even know came up to me and gave me high-fives for my 'excellent takedown', which goes to show that more people would like to stand up to Amber than I thought, even if they don't always have the guts to do it.

Even Daniel seemed impressed. When he called out to me in the corridor after maths, I felt all funny inside. Maybe I'm in love?!

(Also, please note that I didn't even go red . . . Well, I did a bit – but more pink-in-the-cheeks rather than full-on beetroot, so I'll take that as a win.)

At the end of the day, me and Jess left together, just as we had arrived: arm in arm.

As we walked home, we chatted about homework (boring) and boys (she thinks Daniel is cute!) and how long it will be before we end up admitting defeat and putting our Sylvanian Families on eBay out of shame (probs never). It felt so nice and normal.

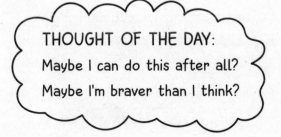

THOUGHT OF THE DAY:
Maybe I can do this after all?
Maybe I'm braver than I think?

FRIDAY 7 JANUARY

Things have been cool at school all week.

Jess and Theo have been teaching me to do keepy-uppies at lunch. I mean, I'm kind of terrible, but I'm getting better. I did five today, which is my personal best.

FYI I'm definitely over Theo now. He's really nice and all, but all he ever talks about is football practice and Arsenal, which is a little bit tedious. I kind of want my first boyfriend to be a man of the world, you know?

I've been chatting to Daniel a bit more and he has LOADS going for him. Aside from the nice smile and cute dimples, he doesn't eat his own boogers, have dirty fingernails or smell like oven food, and those are all big pluses in my book. Oh yeh, and he's kind and funny too.
☺

In other news, things at home are a little bit tense. Dad has to go to Nottingham for a few days next week to do 'important business things'. (No one actually understands what he does for a job, including Mum. It's so boring that we try not to ask questions.)

Mum was not particularly happy about being left on her own at thirty-six weeks pregnant, just in case anything happens. But apparently both me and Toby were born at forty-two weeks. We obviously liked it in her tummy, as she said we had to be practically dragged out.

I think the main problem is that she is so huge now that she is finding it difficult to even move. I honestly don't know why people bother having kids. It seems like a terrible ordeal to me. I mean, look at her. She looks like a human bowling ball, with little arms and legs and a head poking out.

Might be a
bit of an
exaggeration
but not much

SUNDAY 9 JANUARY

I have run into one potential issue with Daniel.

I've been trying to combine our names, in the hope of getting a really cool result, like Kim and Kanyé's 'Kimyé' or Zayn and Gigi's 'Zigi', but the best I could come up with was 'Danottie', which I thought sounded more like a yoghurt drink?!

TUESDAY 11 JANUARY

I was having a lovely dream about being in Little Mix,
when I was rudely awakened by the strangest noise
I ever did hear. It sounded like a cow taking a very
large poo.

Got out of bed to investigate and it turned out it was
actually Mum!

I lightly chastised her for rousing me from my beauty sleep, but apparently that wasn't important right now – because she told me the baby was coming!

'But it's the middle of the night!' I said.

'Babies don't care what time it is!' said Mum.

'Well, that's pretty rude of them. Daytime would be much more convenient.'

She started getting a little frustrated with me, then . . .

LOTTIE I'M ABOUT TO GIVE BIRTH !!

'OK, no need to shout!' I said.

Jeez.

Right, anyway, apparently the baby is also coming very quickly, so I'd better prioritize calling an ambulance over writing in my diary. BRB!!

Note to self: If having a baby makes you moo like a deranged cow, avoid it at all costs.

(5.37 a.m.)

I called an ambulance, but they said they were very busy right now and not quite sure when they will be able to get here.

Then I called Dad and told him to get in the car and drive home real quick.

Mum was shouting some quite unpleasant things about him in the background, but Dad told me not to worry because she always does that when she's in labour.

I really hope Dad and the ambulance hurry up, because the mooing is getting even louder and it's really rather disturbing!

6.53 a.m.

Oh. My. Life.

You will not believe what has just happened.

The baby started coming VERY quickly, and Mum started going VERY red. She was flailing around, arms everywhere. She looked like an angry crab.

The ambulance still hadn't arrived, and Mum said, 'Call 999 again and tell them the baby is coming right now!'

So I did, and the operator said that I would have to help Mum deliver the baby!

YES, YOU DID READ THAT CORRECTLY: I would have to help get the baby out of the angry red crab . . . I mean, Mum.

I was terrified, but the operator talked me through everything, and I did it. I actually did it! I delivered Davina!

I'M NOT GOING TO LIE THOUGH: My eyes saw things I don't think any twelve-year-old should ever have to see.

The ambulance turned up just afterwards. How helpful! Mum had to go to hospital, as Davina was a little premature.

Dad said he'd be home very soon, so I said I'd look after Toby until he arrived.

The best thing is that Dad said we could both have the day off school. Result!

7.14 a.m.

Toby just woke up and came downstairs.

'Sleep well, did you?' I said.

'Yeh, why?' he asked.

Oh, where to begin, Toby, dear boy! I seriously can't believe he didn't hear the mooing.

When Dad arrived home, he took us all to the hospital to see Mum and Davina. The midwife said they are both doing really well, despite Davina being four weeks early, but Mum will probably have to stay in hospital for a little while to make sure.

The midwife also personally congratulated me on delivering my first baby at such a young age. Word had spread quickly across the ward, and a few of the other midwives came over to meet me. I felt like a bit of a celebrity!

I think Mum might have felt a little bit overshadowed by the attention I was getting, but hey – I was the one who did all the hard work.

'About her name, Lottie,' Mum said. 'Are you really set on Davina, because I'm not entirely sure it suits her.'

'No, I couldn't do that to the poor child either,' I said, looking at her perfect little face. 'How about . . . Bella?'

'Oh, I like that. It's lovely! Is that because she's so beautiful?'

'Yes. Yes it is,' I said.

But it was actually because I was starving and Dad had promised to take us to Bella Italia for lunch and all I could think about was the pepperoni pizza with my name on it. I kept that to myself though, as I didn't think Mum and Dad would be so keen on my name choice if they knew it was inspired by a restaurant chain.

'Do you want to hold her, Lottie?' asked Mum.

I took the tiny bundle from Mum's arms and sat on the end of the bed. 'Hello, Bella Brooks,' I said. 'Nice to meet you properly. I'm your big sister, Lottie, and I'm going to help look after you and keep you safe. I think you are going to like being part of our family. We are a bit crazy sometimes, a little shouty and your brother is quite whiffy –'

'Hey!' shouted Toby.

'But we love each other very much, and we are going to love you too.'

I understood now what Mum had being saying about Davina – sorry, I mean Bella Italia. Argh! I mean **BELLA** – completing the family. I didn't get it at first. I thought that maybe they'd forget about me when she came along. But now, holding her in my arms and having been such a big part of her arrival, that's exactly how I felt too.

I felt complete.

THE BROOKS FAMILY

THOUGHT OF THE DAY:
I mean, not to keep going on about it,
but I was pretty amazing today. Not
many people could have kept their calm
in the face of all that blood and gore.
Maybe I'll get a Pride of Britain Award
or something?!

SATURDAY 15 JANUARY

Just after lunch today, Dad shouted up the stairs to me,
'Lottie, can you come down here please?'

'Not really . . . I'm busy doing something incredibly
important right now!' I said.

It *was* true. I was doing something incredibly important.
I was setting up an Instagram account for Professor
Barnaby Squeakington and Fuzzball the 3rd. I'd read an
article about people who'd made thousands of pounds
from their Instafamous pets, and I thought, *I could do
that!* Check out the hammies' solid life advice
@inspirationalhamsters.

237,394 likes

Dad said, 'Well, I think you might find that this quite important too . . .'

So I came downstairs, expecting to find a pile of laundry he wanted me to put away. It took my brain a few seconds to compute the meaning of the big, tangled mass of red hair right in front of me.

'MOLLY? MOLLY! Is that actually you?!'

She didn't say anything at first – she just stood there grinning, her eyes filling with tears. And then, after that brief, emotional moment of silence, we both completely lost it.

After approximately seventeen minutes of ridiculous screaming and hugging and crying, we finally calmed down enough to sit and drink hot chocolate together – mostly made up of marshmallows and cream, of course.

'So why are you back? How come you didn't tell me? What's going on? Are you staying?' I asked – I had so many questions.

'Yes we're back, and yes we're staying! I mean, Australia was great and everything, but we missed our friends and family too much. We even missed the weather . . . We aren't built for the heat.' She pointed at the peeling skin on her sunburnt nose.

'I told you that!'

'I know you did!' she replied, laughing.

'But I don't understand. You said you'd made loads of new friends. What about Isla and the hot surfing instructor – Chad? Or Brad?'

'It wasn't all, strictly speaking . . . true,' she said, looking down. 'I'll really miss Isla, and the beaches are definitely way better in Oz than in Brighton, but fitting in at school wasn't as easy as I made out. And Brad . . . well, he barely knew I existed. I guess I was just jealous of how happy and popular you were back here, while I felt like a total loser.'

It was probably an inappropriate moment to laugh, but I couldn't help it.

'What's so funny?' said Molly, looking a little hurt.

'I saw all your photos on Instagram and I thought exactly the same – that you were having the best time in Oz and not missing me at all! I didn't want YOU to know how lonely I felt or how I was messing everything up.'

'Really?'

'Yes! So I never told you about all the stupid nicknames I got, or about the time I went swimming in a seven-year-old's costume with a tutu, or how I let off a massive trump in PE, or about how I lost all my friends and had to eat my sandwiches alone in the school toilets . . . Oh,

Molly, there is so much I haven't told you!'

Now she was giggling too. 'Well, it doesn't matter, because things are going to be THE BEST from now. I'm starting at Kingswood High as soon as I can get a place!'

'NO WAY!!!'

'YES WAYY!!!'

Then we spent about three hours just chatting and catching up. I told her all about how awesome Jess is, about the whole drama-fest with Amber and Poppy, and about my maybe, possibly, could-be 'thing' with Daniel.

I felt so happy, but also kind of stupid. How did I ever get to the point where I was pretending to be something I wasn't to my own best friend? It just shows you how fake social media can really be.

Just like old times

SUNDAY 16 JANUARY

I have only a couple of pages left. Wow, I can't believe
I've filled up a whole diary! I guess a lot has happened
since we first met, hasn't it?

I feel like I should leave you (and me) with something
deep and meaningful – if I haven't bored you to tears
already and you are still reading, of course! OK,
here goes . . .

Dear Lottie,

*It's me, Lottie. I know this is a bit cringe, writing
to yourself and all, but if I put it all down here
then it might be useful for you to read back later,
just in case you go off the rails and try to reinvent
yourself again.*

FYI, it did not work out!

You've been through a lot in the last few months.

You've grown up a lot, you made new friends (and frenemies), you became a big sister again (wow!) and you got a bra! Still not much to put in it yet, but you are trying not to worry about that too much – there is still plenty of time left for boob growing.

Anyway, let's get back to basics. **THE PLAN!** Well, that went spectacularly wrong! But I'm still glad you did it, because you learnt so much about yourself, didn't you? Here are a few of the things I don't want you (us) to forget.

It's OK to be the quiet one.

It's OK to hang out with whoever you want to.

It's OK if you aren't in the popular gang.

It's OK to wear whatever you like.

It's OK to shave your legs.

It's OK to not shave your legs.

It's OK to be a bit of a geek.

It's OK to be honest.

It's OK to embarrass yourself many times, in many situations, leading to multiple nicknames . . . It's always much worse in your own head.

Finally, and most importantly, (I'm going to underline this one just so we never forget):

It's OK to be you.

Love Lottie xxx

AKA Matey Mc Lobster Legs
AKA Kitkat chunky
AKA Cucumber Girl
AKA Rice Krispie Head
AKA Cute Lil Cupcake

Bye!

DEAR DIARY,

I've finally settled in at Kingswood High, my bezzie Molly is back from Australia, and baby Bella is still too tiny to be as annoying as Toby – result! Surely nothing could go wrong . . . or could it?

READ THE
NEXT DIARY FROM

OUT IN
MARCH
2022!

LOTTIE BROOKS

FOR MORE

EXTREMELY
EMBARRASSING

ADVENTURES!

HOW WELL DO YOU KNOW LOTTIE BROOKS?

Take this quiz to see how much you know about Lottie's extremely embarrassing life.

(1) LOTTIE'S PENCIL CASE IS IN THE SHAPE OF . . .

A A slice of watermelon

B A teddy bear

C A taco

(2) LOTTIE GOES FOR LUNCH. HER SANDWICHES ARE . . .

A Sophisticated coronation chicken

B Posh cucumber

C Classic Marmite

(3) LOTTIE'S ALL-TIME FAVOURITE SINGER IS . . .

A Taylor Swift

B Beyoncé

C Justin Bieber

4 LOTTIE'S TWO PET HAMSTERS ARE CALLED . . .

A   Buggles the Fuzzy and Sandy

B   Sir Barnaby Squeakington and Fuzzball the 3rd

C   Lord Hammy and Wheelie Boy

5 LOTTIE'S FAMILY GOES ON HOLIDAY TO . . .

A   Sunny Beach Caravan Park

B   Rainy Lake Outdoor Retreat

C   Windy Vale Mountain Resort

6 LOTTIE'S LITTLE BROTHER IS CALLED . . .

A   Toby

B   Dave

C   Ethan

7 WHICH OF THESE IS NOT ONE OF LOTTIE'S NICKNAMES?

A   Matey McLobster Legs

B   Lil Cupcake

C   Pasta Princess

FACT FILES BY LOTTIE BROOKS

NAME:
Lottie

STRENGTHS:

* Drawing
* Knowledge of every
  Justin Bieber song ever
* Expert hamster caregiver
* Willpower – was vegetarian for
  a whole day (minus Peperami)

WEAKNESSES:

* VERY easily embarrassed
* Attracts food-related nicknames
* Annoying little brother

NAME:
Jess

STRENGTHS:

* Football
* Brilliant friend
* Confidence in being herself

WEAKNESSES:

* Can't think of any actually . . .

NAME:
Molly

STRENGTHS:

* Amazing best friend
* Surfing

WEAKNESSES:

* Lives far away
* Forgets birthdays

NAME:
Theo

STRENGTHS:

* Being beautiful
* Football
* Being chilled out

WEAKNESSES:

* Football
* Calls me 'Cucumber Girl'

KATIE KIRBY is a writer and illustrator who lives by the sea in Hove with her husband, two sons and dog Sasha.

She has a degree in advertising and marketing, and after spending several years working in London media agencies, which basically involved hanging out in fancy restaurants and pretending to know what she was talking about, she had some children and decided to start a blog called 'Hurrah for Gin' about the gross injustice of it all.

Many people said her sense of humour was silly and immature, so she is now having a bash at writing children's fiction. *The Extremely Embarrassing Life of Lottie Brooks* is her first novel.

Katie likes gin, rabbits, over-thinking things, the smell of launderettes and Monster Munch. She does not like losing at board games or writing about herself in the third person.